Pascal Quignard

Happy the Hours

Last Kingdom XII

Translated by Chris Turner

Hermits United
London • Paris

Published in Great Britain by Hermits United Ltd. 2026

Translated from Pascal Quignard, *Les Heures heureuses*

Printed in France

A catalogue record for this book is available from the British Library
ISBN 978-1-916658-18-9

www.hermits-united.com

Happy the Hours

Contents

Chapter I	Evenings at Compiègne	11
Chapter II	Dying on the Hour	13
Chapter III	Dates and Hours	16
Chapter IV	The Livres d'Heures	24
Chapter V	The Beach at Ischia	30
Chapter VI	There are Three Suns in the Sun	31
Chapter VII	Speculum historiale	36
Chapter VIII	Removal	41
Chapter IX	Hôrai	43
Chapter X	The Yonne	48
Chapter XI	Mogador	54
Chapter XII	The Belém Tower	57
Chapter XIII	Water	63
Chapter XIV	Pavia	67
Chapter XV	The Anarythmetic	69
Chapter XVI	Saint Teresa	75
Chapter XVII	The Master of the Return to Origins	81
Chapter XVIII	The Ruins of Jumièges	86

Chapter XIX	The Lost House	89
Chapter XX	La rue du presbytère	93
Chapter XXI	The Hunt	95
Chapter XXII	The Temple of Time	98
Chapter XXIII	The Cosy Nook for Memories of the World	106
Chapter XXIV	General History	109
Chapter XXV	Skates and Rays	116
Chapter XXVI	Elvers	122
Chapter XXVII	1955–2017	132
Chapter XXVIII	Anger	137
Chapter XXIX	Hero's Tower	148
Chapter XXX	Bern	150
Chapter XXXI	November	153
Chapter XXXII	Dates of Thalassa	160
Chapter XXXIII	Resurgences	168
Chapter XXXIV	Renaissances	171
Chapter XXXV	The Livres d'Heures of Love	176
Chapter XXXVI	The Girl in the Ashes	183

Chapter XXXVII	Poems	188
Chapter XXXVIII	The Palace of Versailles in the Snow in 1991	192
Chapter XXXIX	The 1640s	200
Chapter XL	The Hours Torn from the Book	205
Chapter XLI	Jean Bruneau	208
Chapter XLII	Lucretius	214
Chapter XLIII	Literature as Cryptography	221
Chapter XLIV	Charles de Saint-Évremond	228
Chapter XLV	Giordano Bruno	234
Chapter XLVI	Madeleine de Sablé	238
Chapter XLVII	A Carrot Soup	241
Chapter XLVIII	La Galigaï	246
Chapter XLIX	Spinoza	248
Chapter L	Plutarch	255

Chapter I

At Compiègne, dinner began at seven o'clock. At twenty-five minutes past eight, all would rise from their chairs. At eight-thirty, with supper over, they would leave their coffee cups on the table and file into the drawing-room. The emperor went straight to his study to smoke his cigarette. A minute after he left, the men moved as a body to the smoking-room. The empress stayed with the ladies. As soon as one of the gentlemen came back, the empress's chamberlain would position himself behind a hand-cranked, upright piano; he would begin to turn the handle and go on turning it, uninterrupted, for the rest of the evening. They danced to this shrill, monotonous music. Everyone was bored. Everyone was wondering what time it was. Each of the women asked her neighbour on the bench seats: 'What time is it?' They had to wait until eleven-thirty. At eleven-thirty on the dot, Emperor Napoleon III got up, went over to the empress, took her hand and they retired for the night. As soon as they were through the drawing-room door, Monsieur de Lizan-Marmézis, who was the empress's chamberlain, still standing solemn in his black suit, abruptly let fall the crank-handle.

All was quiet.

Everyone went to bed.

Chapter II

Dying on the Hour

On Friday 14 December 1591, at the age of forty-nine, John of the Cross died at Úbeda.

Twelve friars, each with a candle in hand, stood around in tight array, his cell being so narrow.

Six friars on the right, six on the left.

Before he died, he asked the friars surrounding him: 'What hour is it?'

One thought it would soon be midnight.

But John shook his head.

'It isn't midnight because at that hour I shall stand before our Lord and I shall be saying matins.'

The friars on the right-hand side began to shudder with sadness.

Another hastily opened his breviary. He sought out the prayer for the commendation of the dying. But the ailing John noticed and, in his gentle voice, told him: 'Brother, put aside your breviary for the love of God. My body is in a state of prayer. I think we should all be quiet now.'

Father Alonzo pointed out that it was Friday. If he were so fortunate as to die now, before Saturday came, he would enjoy the Sabbatine Privilege of the Scapular of Carmel. In other words, the Virgin Mary would free him swiftly from Purgatory as he ascended to heaven.

Brother John gave a little spluttering laugh and said: 'Father, I have just told you I shall be saying matins at midnight.'

All the friars on the left began to weep behind their hands.

John of the Cross sat up. He slid his fingers under his pillow and pulled out a packet of letters he had been keeping beneath his head all those days.

He spoke the name of Father Bartholomew of Saint-Basile and asked him for his candle.

Father Bartholomew handed it over and Brother John set about burning the packet in front of everyone.

Once it had properly caught fire, he dropped it on the tiled floor of his cell, where the paper burned up completely.

When there was just a little pile of ash on the floor, he commanded them: 'Go back to your cells now. It's time to close the monastery.'

The friars on the right filed out. The friars on the left followed. They can be heard bolting the doors. They get into bed in their cells and pull the blankets up to their chins. They sleep.

Brother John himself takes a little rest while Father Alonzo watches over him.

Suddenly the clock of the Chapel of the Saviour strikes midnight.

'What are they ringing?' asks Brother John opening his eyes at the sound of the first strokes.

When Father Alonzo replies that it is matins, he exclaims joyfully:

'Glory to God! I take my leave.'

He puts his lips to the crucifix in his hands; he calmly recites the prayer *In manus tuas, Domine, commendo spiritum meum*. Into the fingers of thy hands, Master, I deliver the breathing of my breath. He has not time to get to *meum* as he expires on the hour. The author of *Dark Night* is dead before the bells of daybreak have finished ringing.[i]

Chapter III

Dates and Hours

Saint John of the Cross does not say *meum* as he dies, for there is no 'me' in death. There is no identity in death. Neither language nor, indeed, any world outlives the breath that flowed out all at once in death. It is even the case that, inside the living language we learn so slowly from the lips of our mothers and grandmothers in childhood, all that words cannot reach is lost, for only what is remembered can be summoned. And only what we do not have before our eyes needs to be evoked by its name. The past is simply that evocation, not a state of things. Even history is only that evocation, a wild beast's hunger, bloody slaughter, hope for a respite or a renascence, an avenger's desire.

Even thought waits; it waits constantly. It is, for its part, a waiting on its source. It is merely the reflux of the dreams it takes back into its maw and seeks to gulp down.

Then the breath evaporates from each letter as the

characters are written.

The letter is what isolates a returning silhouette, which it makes sparkle in the depths of the soul, now returned to silence.

Behind the letter, lastly, stands the date, which marks the gulping-down. Less than a silhouette, the date is a marker for what has vanished.

Thus, behind the *littera*, wherein lies the lost element, stands the *datum* – the given. What the datum was in the real.

In this book, in which I wish to take leave of the letter, I need to gather these last vestiges: figures and dates. The hours that bring them together.

*

What is a date? A date is the minimal unit of history. The moment when the story begins. The state of the given when the body emerged into external space.

The date is to history what the proper name is to genealogy. It is the mark of death falling on a child being born, in the distress of its origin, a mark waiting within that child, in terror of its death agony.

What is a tomb? A body beneath a stone.

What is written on that stone? A name and a date.

*

Even mourning, in which desire has however lost its object, still waits.

Mourning is the waiting that no longer quite understands what it is waiting for but which, in an absolute sense, waits.

For the dead man dies longer than his death, in the same way as life precedes the child being born in the course of an actual life.

Within the reckoning of figures and the sequence of numbers, the hour, day and month of the year of birth constitute the date when the subject's life begins – he who, in fact, has lived much longer than the time spent in the atmosphere, much longer than language, breath, the group and the society grant him.

If the date of birth is a given in the course of the unforeseeable gift of physical time from which human time borrows, a given that draws upon the speed of light in the sky, baptism brings the dead into the names of the living, on the pages of the register of births or parish records. The revenant *revient* – that is to say, comes back – suddenly joining 'here' to 'now' in a little salt and water on a body that cries out when, as it comes into atmospheric air, gasping for breath, it discovers the group on the Earth.

The combination of one datum with preceding ones is an attempt to tame the irreversible, irreproducible uniqueness of each event. This entanglement positions it as part of a vaster diachronic thrust which, left to itself, would be not just excessive but, above all, dispersive. This second molecule, subservient to the first atom that is the date, is called sentence or sequence or life or period or epoch or legend or myth. Such is the minimal storyline.

This is how history wrests the *datum* from unnameable contingency. It is how the father extirpates the small body from the dark waters of the great genesic maternal body. It is how the patronymic and forename already pass on and incise what will be carved on the surface of the little marble, or granite, or wooden, monument of the tomb; it is how the family chronicle rearranges figures; clearly distinguishes names, sentences, and ultimately chapters: that is to say, families. On a piece of paper, it stacks the branches of a tree: that is to say, it piles up storylines one upon another; it never retains them all; and it wipes away whole swathes of the past as it builds its family romances. The date then becomes the equivalent of what the name is vis-à-vis words: an ancestor is back. Linguistics was first a genealogy. Once a name had been freed up by a dead relative, a child was no longer exposed.

The infant was allowed to live so that that dead person could return. At that moment a strange similitude is *added* to the given, to its more or less shapeless physical resemblances, and it transfigures them. Faced with the new, after assigning it to one of the ancestors' patronymics, after sacrificing it in the forename of a martyred saint,[ii] reproduction always says, as it leans over the wailing infant to take stock of him:

'It's amazing how like his grandfather he is.'

'Don't you think he's more the spitting image of his maternal uncle?'

*

But dates are much more than what names are in relation to words. They are much more than markers of emergence and destruction with respect to the basic destiny which this ecclesiastical computation downgrades, exiling the origin into the opacity of the flesh.

Dates stand opposed to hours.

For there remains, behind the horizon of their world, behind the constitution of their annals, a time that does not belong to the languages of humans, nor to the tales they tell, nor to the sentences that express them, nor to the rules of grammatical tenses that encode them. It is the time that passes back and forth in the sky, whose words and pronouncements, whose *fata* and fays, are the hours. The *Horae* of Rome, the *Hôrai* of the Greeks do not belong to the world of mortals. The *Hôrai* referred to the inhuman seasons which lay down the rhythm of their duration for all nature's creatures and events on the surface of the Earth. It is the time that allows (physical) nature to flourish and the time that precedes (cosmic) life, which is born and ebbs and flows with the movement of the ocean tides and follows the disposition of the stars on the imaginary vault of the sky. It is the time which, first on Earth, then in life, issuing forth from the depths of the heavens, underlies the immense cycle of the seasons, going further back than any of the tiny sequences that human beings hitch to it.

*

Behind the hours are the landscapes.

The time that stands behind time is the rotation of landscapes.

Spring, summer, autumn, winter.

Landscapes are the unforgettable faces of original physical time.

If the Hours are the heirs to primordial cosmic time, 'time' – tempus – is then placed back within its own 'tempest'.

The Hours are the individual squalls of that original raging tempest.

They designate the movements of the time of the Erstwhile, whose explosion in the heart of the heavens continues in spatial form in proportion to the speed of the streams of light running through it, which spurt out so violently in the storm, and fizzle so delightfully behind the greenery of the landscape, or above the mountain peaks, or within the changing clouds.

To put it as the ancient Greeks did, the enigma (*ainigma*) specific to each hour is engendered by the existence of the seasons, from which nature (*physis*) offered itself to the living animals (*ta zōa*) from the world of the immense primal sea (*panthalassa*).

These time spans of Physis precede the times of Being.

It is in this area beyond Being that the enigma specific to the seasons – to the landscapes of life – emerges in the depths of stellar night.

To put it in more modern terms, the *Erstwhile – le Jadis*, 'the past before what came to pass' – accumulates silence, obscurity and depth, while the *Past* encrypts the mythic, the biographical, the legendary.[iii]

Had Alexander the Great not invaded Persia and India, had Caesar not reformed the calendar and invented dictatorship, had Augustus not imposed the principate over the whole of the known Earth, Bonaparte would not have been 'first consul' and would not have crowned himself 'emperor'.

Thus, there is a metempsychosis of nations through the languages from which they receive their myths.

Thus, there is a metamorphosis of all the forms that have the original explosion as their direct fountainhead.

Or, rather than a metempsychosis: a psychosis.

Or, rather than a metaphysics: a physics.

Or, rather than a metamorphosis: a morphosis – a continuous, cosmic, then thalassal, then biotic, then vegetal, then animal, then human – morphosis, which repatriates things to the original night, as it repatriates us to the flesh which language represses.

Chapter IV

The Livres d'Heures

Forms immediately swallowed back down into hell, forms adorned with gilded edges.

In the books my grandmother kept in the bottom of the cupboard set aside for children, at child height, mixed in with the series of novels written by the Comtesse de Ségur in the 1850s in the forêt de l'Aigle, in her fine chateau some 15 miles from the village of Verneuil, books bound in a soft cover of frayed pink fabric (tea-rose pink, old-rose pink), there was a battered little square, ivory-coloured, cardboard-bound volume that was light, fascinating, crisp in its pages: the *Livre d'heures* of the Duc de Berry. The illustrations were affixed separately to each page; some had come adrift from the page they were meant to be stuck to. These miniatures were so precious, spare, and stunning in their fragility and detail that, even as a child, I handled them with great care.

Into the wide-open jaws of the jet-black maw of Hell,

the chalky, naked bodies of women were falling, their white breasts drooping, their mouths wide open as they screamed. The men, grey and naked, with their bellies and upturned sexual organs on display, were sliding upside down into the abyss, their arms outstretched toward the flames licking up from the bottom of the page – flames in which all would soon be engulfed.

*

In the hall of a magnificent chateau, before the fire blazing in a huge hearth, a large woven-iron screen provides protection from sparks and stray embers.

Two little dogs run around among the dishes on the table, suddenly sticking out their tongues to get a taste of them.

Jean de France, Duke of the Province of Berry, is sitting at the table, wearing a blue, gold-embroidered robe and a fur hat.

It is winter.

Jean de France, duc de Berry, was a collector of Hours.

In the study of his palace at Bourges were fifteen *livres d'heures* that he had in his possession.

Happy hours. Hours of the fecund or fertile rotation of time. Calendars designed for each day's private prayers. Landscapes, scenes associated with religious vows, were themselves associated with the more or less misty, damp, profuse, irradiated moments which the sun afforded to the various chateaux that the prince possessed. Silhouettes obedient to each call the season makes. For each day has its particular colour; has its celebratory gleam for every dawn; has its shadow of penitence and shame for every evening; has its abrupt tears of death and divine passion, of birthday celebration, of rebirth and rushing forth anew.

*

Saint Paul wrote: *Vetera transierunt sed omnia nova.* Though old things may age, all things are new.[iv]

The past passes but, since it does nothing but depart, all things spring up brand new in their beginnings. The past revolves on itself; unable to remain in space, it yet puts no roots down anywhere; driven by a dizzying whirl, a rotation whereby what falls mysteriously rises again. Every childhood is a dawn. Every dream is a dawn. Every image is a dawn. Every new thing is naked.

It is the end of spring. It is the month of June.

They are swimming, grey creatures that they are, like spermatozoa, like translucent tadpoles.

The men dive stark naked into the waters of the Seine, by the riverbank beside the new Sainte-Chapelle, by the orchard of the blessed King Louis.[v]

We are at the height of summer. It is August. The peasants, with their tunics tucked up into their belts, are reaping, harvesting, baling.

In the river, dark men and pale women, having laid down their coloured clothing and shifts on the bank, are bathing, drenched in light, beside the Château d'Étampes.

*

When he had reached the end of his days, Duke Jean de Berry took as his new motto 'Le temps verra': time will see.

But where does time see?

Time sees in the hours.

The colours were ground with a pestle on a marble surface. Then they were moistened with water mixed with gum, so that they would stick to and become ingrained in the porous, smooth calfskin or buckskin of the page.

There is a hierarchy in elation.

The sky was always done first in a painting. Then the backgrounds. Then the landscapes.

Then one sets about the foreground and the figures were limned out.

Hands were given form last; faces sketched out and given relief.

Paul de Limbourg liked to do the scenes, Jean Colombe the faces.

*

The illustration symbolising winter shows first a bare tree in snow.

Then a sheepfold with its huddled flock.

In front of three barrels of wine, magpies, rooks and jays are pecking at imaginary seed, searching for it beneath the settled layer of snow.

A man is entering the farmyard, covering his mouth with the flap of his cloak.

In the far distance, on the snowy path at the top of the miniature, a peasant, seen from behind, is beating a donkey laden with wood as it climbs in this wintry time.

Die schneyichte Zeit: the time that is only snow – that is what this hour is.

On the left of the image, however, if the eye lingers a moment, a man in a red turban and a woman in a black coiffe are sitting peaceably in front of a fire, beneath a tall wooden structure covered with a very thick layer of snow. Their legs are splayed, though not touching, and the sodden tunic of each is hitched up, revealing their very different genitals as they warm them by the crackling fire in the hearth.

How these images thrilled me as a child! And how the snow worked its fascination on my childhood!

Beside the flames, a cat, itself white as the snow falling in the picture, is turning its head to stare at the two very distinct sexes displayed by the woman and the man, both in a slumbrous state, neither dilated nor erect.

Chapter V

The Beach at Ischia

We traced our path by the sea's rollers. Darkness was flooding the sky. M. and I advanced more and more slowly, it being scarcely possible to see. We followed the fringe of spume as it sparkled in the night, the way snails follow the silvery trace of their slime. In the blackness – against the black sand of the volcano – we found the cheap eateries with their fried vegetables, their aubergines sliced amazingly thin, their many-coloured peppers and Lucca olives, and to the fish restaurants where they fried cuttlefish, squid, prawns, *pasta alle vongole*, tiny soles and fresh anchovies barely seared in sputtering oil.

Happy – infinitely happy – hours.

Chapter VI

There are Three Suns in the Sun

Dusk in the day is what autumn is in the year.

Autumn is the name for when the moon is closest – so close – to the Earth, just as spring took from the flowers the image of an emerging flower. Winter is snow in much the same way as summer is distilled in the song of the cuckoo. These pairings are inseparable. They precede us. They form us. They alert us. They alternate. They revolve. Time on the grand scale revolves. The hours, unlike dates, revolve. The finest part of time resolves itself into these images that are older than humans. Both things revolve. As do the stars. A flower peeping out from the snow is what the robin suddenly hymns in the cold of a winter's night beneath a low-hanging moon. The world is more circular than linear. It is the sun flowers rise towards to consume its light. It is life the roses, peonies and dahlias bring into being as they devour that sunlight.

*

The only flowers that grow in winter,
O huge drooping flowers in white, tinged with a little pink,
hellebores,
anemones of the dead,
tall flowers on the dead lawn or rather the fallow ground,
or down in the black mud,
with their leaves so enormous, thick and dark,
their stamens as black as the ink cuttlefish exude under the sea,
flowers which grow when the cold comes,
which were once called Christmas roses!

*

Flowers that grow in the loam which gets covered in pellets of ice,
which shrinks back then cracks,
its cracks filling with ice.
Flowers that do not freeze even in the worst of winter.
That go on growing in the layer of snow they peep through.

*

Upon waking on Easter Sunday, every woman and man should throw their windows wide open. Every woman and man should close their eyes very, very tight. You should open them again right away and, at that very moment, stare as hard as you can at the sun as it dances in its dawning. For it so happens that three suns, three suns as a trinity, in their glory, burst forth all at once, simultaneously, on that day – that Sun-day, that *Sonn-tag*, that day of Resurrection, that day of renewal in the strange golden circle formed by the star at the source of our world as it spins out the dizzying whirl we call Time.

This old custom is attested in 1255 in Burgundy and was still current in 1933 in the Yonne. In the first sun, all the life and death of the god are behind us. It is a string of scenes we know by heart, scenes of a fairytale nature. Like a Book of Hours in which the delicate miniatures pass successively before our eyes, provided that Good Friday has awakened them and the Sunday of Resurrection has spooled them out again. Darkness, cold and hunger, thorns and whips, the byre and the brazier, winter and the whole dead year are pitched more into the abyss of the past than into memory and its words, its fetishes, its recollections. Daybreak has become the dawning of a new year.

The second sun marks the blessing of the cattle at the manger, the mares in the stable, the sows in the pigpen, the poultry in the henhouse, the bees in the hives, the married couples in their beds at dawn. On Easter Sunday morning, custom has it that the mistress of the house should lie abed in a state of cleanliness, entirely naked. She covers her breasts with her right arm. She conceals her vulva with her cupped left hand. Only the priest enters the marital bedroom; he leaves the choir and altar boys at the door. The mistress of the house then opens her arms and removes her hand. The priest raises his and blesses her womb with the aspergillum, that it may be fertile, and her breasts, that they may give plentiful milk.

During that time, in the main room, on the tablecloth for the Easter meal, the servant girls lay out the silver-gilt knife and fork that the master of the house will alone be allowed to use when the Sunday lunch begins as the chapel bell strikes midday. Only on this day does he have use of them.

After the Easter meal, people come out from their homes, leaving their paddocks, hives and farms behind. Following the priest, the altar boys in their albs, the choirboys singing their psalms, and the brass band, its instruments alternating with as yet unbroken voices singing hymns, parade across the fields, blessing them. They come to the forest, which they also bless. Then all process to the well to bless its waters. This brings them all into the third sun: suddenly, spring is here, ringing, streaming, fluttering, whinnying, blushing, radiant; no further need for prayers or priest. All is one unanimous song. All are part of one long round dance. And so the year has reappeared, society is reproduced, nature is reborn.

*

At Le Havre I came in by the Porte de l'Eure. I could see the donkey, the bell, the barn, the mill, the fountain. Or at least their ghosts in the stones. This was the city beneath the city. It was the old town from before 1525, before the *Male marée*, the calamitous tide.[vi]

Chapter VII

Speculum historiale

There is an illustration by Paul de Limbourg that I prefer to all those in the Duc de Berry's book. It is the most beautiful of all, the most finely wrought, the most lavish. I put it on the cover of one of my *Last Kingdom* volumes, the fourth, entitled *Les Paradisiaques*. Eve is naked and standing over Adam, who is kneeling on the green grass. In her right hand she holds the wonderful scarlet fruit she has plucked from the branch. What moves me, however, is something unconnected with this offering that will be the prelude to sexual damnation. The moving element in the picture is her left hand: the naked young woman has her left hand resting gently, lovingly, on the naked man's shoulder, because she loves him. We cannot tell if she is caressing the base of his neck to express her love, leaning on him from sheer friendship and trust, or squeezing the flesh of his shoulder to have him take the fruit she holds out in her open palm; but most notably, she is looking anxiously, with a pained expression, into the eyes of the man who has turned his face toward her.

As for the man, it is only her that he sees. He is not looking at the fruit. He is drowning in her gaze.

*

Vincent of Beauvais wrote: Adam and Eve committed their sin on the very day of their creation.

It was, therefore, the sixth day after the genesis of the world.

Noon is the hour that falls right at the heart of the day. That falls straight down on to the Earth.

Since the sin took place on the twelfth stroke of the twelfth hour, nudity – the *shame* of nudity – is dated to the thirteenth hour.

A sense of bodily modesty immediately overcomes man, in such a way as to separate him from all the other animals, in the radiance of noon, as the ringing of bells marks the most intensely lit part of the day. Shame, which appeared at the thirteenth hour, is what attests to the Fall. Man immediately uses his hand to cover his sex, which he hides from the gaze of the first woman, who looks on him henceforth with a kind of suspicion or fear.

A couple of hours pass. Then another. Twilight is more or less upon them. She hides her two breasts beneath her left arm. She conceals her sex beneath the palm of her right hand.

At last, in the fully twilit hour of the sixth day, the man and the woman are driven out. Crossing the threshold, they moaned and groaned. But as soon as they left Eden, they did something worse than lamenting or expressing regret: they spoke. And as soon as they left Eden, she took her hand from his shoulder; friendship disappeared; sexual hostility appeared; and they *dialogued*, which means that opposition between persons, division between genders, antagonism of poles and roles and war were everywhere.

This is why, at the point of the reparation of this world, the redemption of sin in this world, Jesus is nailed to the cross at noon.

*

The previous evening, beneath the moon, by an old ruined well in an olive grove, a kneeling God had whispered to his disciples as they slept all around him, their backs leaning against the trunks of the olive trees or the old grey stones:

'What, could ye not watch with me *one hour*?'

*

Agostino Inveges does not see the chronology of Genesis the way Vincent of Beauvais does.

Agostino Inveges calculates the hours differently, those first moments the first man and the first woman lived while still in Paradise. He studies the original mathematics more deeply. Agostino Inveges writes: the Earth was created on 22 March, a Tuesday, in the first quarter of the first hour of the day, just as the sun was rising.

Eve sinned on Friday 25 March at eleven, twisting off the apple, which sparked her desire more than it did her curiosity, and even more than it did her hunger, from the end of the branch where it hung.

Adam bit into it, in his turn, at midday exactly.

It was at that precise moment of the sun's zenith that man was unable to swallow; it was at that moment that the piece of apple got stuck in his throat, bulging from his neck as the first remnant of time, obstructing deglutition.

The first remnant of time is the *Adam's apple*: it is anxiety, which gives you a lump in the throat, residing just below language.

As for God, it is clearly stated that he did not walk in the garden until three in the afternoon.

The first woman, both her arms upraised and howling, followed by the first man, both hands closed over his eyes, his right foot still planted in what tiny space remains of Paradise, are expelled from the Garden at four.

Chapter VIII

Removal

The past is immediately transformed the moment we arrive at a new place. With each change of home, a new wave instantly floods through the whole of our life. In what is being discovered, our entire memory is dramatically reset on the basis of what comes back to mind.

*

As it goes up, all new architecture radically robs us of a place that once was.

*

I doubt that the Sacred Congregation of Rites was right, on 6 July 1940, to permit the electrification of the lamp over the tabernacle. A strange thing to be concerned about when Germany had just seized control of France. At the moment when Franco was invading Tangier.

*

Behind every nest, there is a broken shell.

Chapter IX

Hôrai

Hora describes that movement which hastens time. That which ex-horts and in-curvates. *Hora* is the *driver-out-of-the-garden* (hortus). It is what impels the thrust of time at the exit from Eden. At the exit from the mother.

On the ships of antiquity, the *hortator* was the man tasked with setting the rhythm for the rowers.

This is the role Orpheus performs on the first ship – the vessel commanded by Jason as he heads for the Black Sea in search of the Golden Fleece. And it is this rhythm-setting that Butes, the true musician, detests – Butes who then jumps into the sea.

Hence, hour (*hora*) describes what calls on time to hasten (*hortor*) in the interior of its coming. It is not, in any way, that the hour encourages time to be on time. *Hora* strives to make the inflow in the landscape flow in. It pushes it to be ahead of itself. *Hora* urges time not 'to be on time', but to 'return within time' always as the first time, as *primum tempus* or *printemps* (spring), as beginning of time, as emergence of both *natura* and *nascentia* – nature and birth.

This is how *Hora* hides the secret name that Rome was at pains never to disclose to its enemies: *Flora*.

Flora is the secret name of time.

The budding and flowering of the hour is the great goddess of life who conquers wintry death. Who brings under her law the crisis-ridden time in the depths of the December night (the Saturnalia, the festival of Saturn/Chronos, putting to death the god or king of the old year). Flora transforms into Hora so as not to sully the name of the goddess. Flora is the divinity who, in giving the hour (*heure*, *hora*) to the Earth – that is to say, in gifting it the seasons – brings spring to the time whose father is storm. The divinity who resuscitates nature in the polychrome, multi-coloured, motley, unpredictable outpouring that is the *Floralia* of the Eternal City.

*

As the day is born, the white waterlily is the first to open.

At seven comes the St. John's wort.

At eight, it is the turn of the pimpernel.

At nine, the marigold...

This is how Carl Linnaeus began to devise his wonderful clock.[vii]

*

Birdsong, with its modulations, itself occurs at regular hours. Flights, sounds, sequences, the tops and bottoms of the bushes, the leaves of the treetops mark passing time and distribute it across the site. The crowing of the cockerel is an (expergefactive) alarm-clock; the cry of the eagle owl (*bubo*) is a sigh (*gemulus*); that of the screech owl (*ulula*) a lament (*querulus*); that of the little owl (*noctua*) a cooing (*intortus*) which loops back on itself; the song of the cicada is a strident cry (*obstreperus*); that of the swallow a shrill whistle (*peragula*).

The song of the nightingale – in other words, the song of the innocent little boy whose mother has cut his throat and served him up to his father in a stew – is heard in the middle of the night.[viii]

*

In Fragment 100, which is so radical, Heraclitus writes: 'the seasons bring all things.'

Horas hai panta pherousi.

Word for word: the hours all things bring.

The hours bring budding, ripening, withering, and becoming-other.

Nothing of what becomes escapes the *horaison* of the hour.

For men are not mortals, they are ultimates. In their hands all things come to an end. In the language that evokes their world, all is lost. Everything comes last in the ephemerality of the discontinuous days. All grows endlessly dark in the inchoative succeeding darknesses, night after night, up to the moment when everything in the world passes away in the depths of their dying gaze.

*

In Sophocles, the most valiant of all the Greek warriors, Ajax, with the sword of his death in his hand says at line 646 of the tragedy that bears his name: 'The vast, countless years give rise to all things invisible and, once they have appeared, conceal them inside the very light that makes them manifest to us. There is, thus, nothing one cannot expect'.[ix]

Ajax, the bravest of the warriors of Greece, says boldly: Everything is to be expected from expectant waiting.

What happens – for time is *what happens* – is not subordinate to an order and not subject to a fate.

It is the Unforeseeable.

The only thing that dominates in the past is the upsurge without mantic power (without prophecy, without future) that returns endlessly, insofar as it does not return as it will have been.

Such is the Hour: nothing one truly lives through is narratable.

*

In the *Odyssey*, *Canto* XI, when Ulysses has descended into the blood-rimmed trench, when he enters the Underworld – introduced into the mouth of Hades by Tiresias the Shaman, the master of the shadows, the only mortal who has been both sexes, the only body that has experienced the two pleasures, the only dead man who has not tasted of the waters of Lethe and, hence, still retains a memory of his days on Earth – and approaches the shade of Ajax, Ajax bearing still in his hand the sword of his suicide, turns his back defiantly on the legendary, cunning warrior. He refuses to speak to him. He refuses to speak to the speaker. Pure silence among the shades.

Chapter X

The Yonne

The morning arrives not radiantly but invisibly, making things appear. It precedes the red disc of the star. The morning imperceptibly snuffs out the shape of the moon, not yet entirely faded from the sky. Its freshness begets the clouds that are delineated in the sky as it opens out. Its whitening ushers in the half-light, the penumbra that yields to stronger shadows and brings a gleam to the edges of the tiled roofs, to the waters of the Yonne as they flow by, and to the first waves rippling across it as the wind gets up. The pale blue of the clump of thistles appears, then the dog rose with its small red seed pods, the house, all the little occupants of the riverbank, the black, flat-bottomed boat and the hazel trees. In its paleness the dawn still unifies the shadowless entities. Suddenly, the extreme pallor of the stars fades into minute points, little *puncta*, *punctula*, *punctilla* against the celestial vault. The sun's first rays arrive within the dawn. Those rays disrupt the outlines of things; as they shine, they strip away the nocturnal darkness that robbed things of their colour, that deformed them, united them, fused them together. If daybreak gives way to those first rays, they in turn give way to the morning: in a brief instant that is merely a tiny fragment of the hour, the risen sun rises in the sky, picks out shapes on the Earth, dehumidifies them, surrounds them with repercussions of shade that lie beyond silence, with weakness and even with mist, which the first heat of the star creates by transforming the water's surface into steam. Dawn does not bring with it colour. True colour comes not even with morning but with day. Dawn is no more day than morning is first light. Dawn, *aube*, *alba*, still in the night, is that *whitening* ahead of all the colours that *white* perhaps contains.

Dawn is the Erstwhile of colours that appears in the sky before they resuscitate.

*

When the sun sets over the river, it is not yet dusk, but evening. When the sun departs, it goes away like this: it begins to take its leave of the garden at the alder trees just beyond the anglers' wooden bridge. Every evening, there, to the right of the hazel thicket, before you get to the apple tree, it plunges down irresistibly.

A moment of light persists before all falls dark.

A little pocket in which the strange light resists, before disintegrating – the light which Fontenelle, who believed in nothing, attributed to God.

The old, centenarian philosopher, who did not believe in God, said that, between evening and night, after sundown, before the dusk, God had 'granted a moment of grace'.

The hour called *entre chien et loup* – between dog and wolf – refers to a moment when you cannot distinguish between the silhouettes of neighbouring or related species. What differentiates them is lost. The hour between kids and lambs. Plants melt into one another. The original formlessness swallowing up all the forms of physical, natural, living beings: such is *le crépuscule* – the dusk.

And so, in addition to the crepuscular hour, there is a light that appears, beyond the horizon, after the sun has sunk below it. It is the vesperal hour. It is this aura that marks it off from the hour of dusk. It is this grace of which Fontenelle speaks strangely.

*

If the auroral hour is the sublime hour of appearance, the crepuscular hour, more subtle, is that of dis-pearence.

The boreal is the surprising elevation at the pole, when luminescence is projected into the upper atmosphere long before the sun comes over the horizon.

The vesperal is the hour of a kind of sorrow at dying.

It is a ghost.

Vesper is a star difficult to spot, that can be made out only gradually, deep in the twilit sky, while the old Latin words *creper* and *creperus* refer to that moment in visible reality when every shape grows uncertain.

Crepuscular is the name for the rapturous time of the day. It brings us closer to happiness, to sleep, to embraces, to dreams. It is the hour when the lamps are lit in every closed place. Everywhere. In houses, in living rooms, on all the altars, in all the side chapels, when the sun has departed this world.

Vespers refers to the most solemn of the canonical hours, being the moment set aside in the night time for the dead god.

It is the concert hour.

It is the hour when melancholia finds confirmation in *the darkness that is being born.*

When *languor* seeps into a body suddenly enfeebled.

There comes the ring of bells in the distance, over

the heath
   or over distant hills,
   for vespers. At that sound, the sky unleashes
   the shade of evening.

And there rings out the strange stellar event which spreads the invisible.

*

Forms tremble inwardly before sloughing off their skins, their casings, their habitual contours. All the light has at last vanished before the lunar and stellar gleams appear – that is to say, before the celestial fall of night in person: the goddess Night. The night, by which I mean blue night, nocturnal darkness, that is not total blackness.

*

The universe is not alive.

*

Her whole life long, Emily Dickinson refused to learn to tell the time from a pocket watch or a clock face. She did not understand the to-ing and fro-ing of the different hands. She said the church bells were quite enough for her and, beyond that, the sun in the sky told her all she needed to know.

Chapter XI

Mogador

Ten kilometres from Mogador, behind the highest rock on the shore but before the saint's white tomb, on the side permanently shaded by the cliff, were two grey wooden beach huts. They had once been white. The rain had faded them and covered them with a kind of salt, a coating of salt, season after season, that had gnawed away at them. The wood had turned grey, pale, mellow. It was there she went to change, closing the porous door behind her and putting the latch back down, her feet in the coolness of the sand and stone, in a warm scent of argan wood. The wooden cabins, which seemed to back up against the mountain, were in fact partially incrusted in the rock. They were tended to by the hotel keeper. She kept watch over them, reserving them exclusively for women. Suddenly I saw M. emerge quietly, walking slowly on the sand. First in the distance, then nearer, then right in front of me as I continued to read, stretched out in a deck chair that the beach attendant had set up at the edge of the wet sand.

She was heading for the sea.

Three or four times a day, she was irresistibly drawn to the sea. I cannot express how emotional I still feel about this. It is much more than just a memory. Every day, for hours, she either swam or walked in the water. The rest of the time she read, or scanned her mobile for places to eat or new places to visit along the coast or on the moorland behind it.

Arriving near the sea, she would suddenly throw off her robe at the edge of the dry sand, leaving her long, black, curly hair to tumble over her shoulders as she went on walking rather mechanically into the shallow water and the waves at the edge. Strictly speaking, she slid into the ocean. She slipped impassively into the freezing, always rather windswept waters of the vast, rippling Atlantic as though the water were air. How I admired her. How touching were her bold gestures. Going straight into the sea when it was colder than snow itself. The Atlantic Ocean's waves, tipped white with foam, bristled at her gradual approach. The wind would suddenly hurl the rollers against her belly or breasts. She did not flinch. When at last the water was up around her navel and stomach, she slipped in, her chin held very high, and made for the open sea.

In the distance, far in the distance, she would climb up on to one of the rocky outcrops of the old fort that were too far out for my abilities as a swimmer. I never swam out to join her there. The water beat violently against the faintly gleaming, almost imperceptible rock. Her body was a small point surrounded by great white sheaves of spray. A point at the end of the world, in the ocean.

*

There are women whose souls are burning embers.

*

Time passed without answering for its endless flight.

Chapter XII

The Belém Tower

The sound of the sea is thunderous. A deafening of the soul. The past keeps returning in the form of strange waves, which are never alike. Which drench and soak.

They can knock you to the ground.

We are bombarded by the past of our lives and, in the depths of living matter, by the past of nature upon the Earth.

*

I waited for her for hours on the shores of the Aegean Sea. Of the Tyrrhenian Sea. Of the Adriatic. The Atlantic Ocean. The English Channel. At least twice a day, I waited for Emmanuèle, who had short, brown hair.

I waited for her on the rocks.

Amid the seaweed.

On the dunes.

I lost sight of her in the rolling waves.

After an hour or two I grew anxious. I told myself: 'Perhaps Emmanuèle has gone across the bay to have breakfast at Barbara Cassin's.' I was worrying to no purpose. I was elsewhere. Still in 'a place beyond place'. It is an autistic trait I retain from my childhood. Suddenly I melt into nature. I walk on, but my soul has vanished in the course of my walking. I move like a sleepwalker impervious to danger. I lose myself in what I write in the way I lose myself in intoxication in the evening.

*

It isn't the arts that count, it's giving oneself up to the forces on which the world is grounded, the thrusts that precede even life.

The sea precedes life.

*

She was climbing and anxiety was rising with her.

The path is steep. We are climbing right up at the top of Mount Sintra. There is heavy mist. We have pushed on through the increasingly damp forest and entered the cloud enshrouding the peak. Its humidity weighs heavily.

Her breath was heaving. It was coming out strangely.

She was suffocating. It was the eruption of the volcano.

The powerful fear rising at Emmanuèle's core.

Strange vent of birth. Strange fits of breathlessness that had replaced the sobbing. These were genuine fulminations, outbursts, outbreaks, blazing releases of anger, of light.

Even in language, there are fissures.

Even in nature, everything speaks, crackles, shouts, sings.

*

So many filthy words streaming out as the extraordinary improvisations of fury inevitably, magically, inspired them.

*

It was in the month of March that the world was created. In the month of March that Jesus was conceived. March was the first month the star shed its light on when the gods took a hand in inventing the Golden Age on Earth. It was March 1997, we were with Emmanuèle at the Belém Tower.

Then M., Em. and I had to take the car. It wasn't even a coastal path. There was one rock after another, but also concrete blocks piled up above the sea. The wind blew and swirled so hard that it snatched our words away. This all made an enormous din. The sea hurled its waves against the rocks below. We had to skirt round houses that looked out directly on to the Atlantic. The waves were exploding beneath the concrete sea walls.

Walking along the coast turned out to be more than difficult on account of there being no path, on account of the strength of the wind. Nevertheless, there too she dived.

It was seemingly something she could not resist.

She did not so much dive as fly off her hinges.

I remember one day we were at a restaurant, having come over from Saint-Énogat to the marina at Dinard by the coastal route. We were eating cuttlefish, drinking an aperitif on the small balcony of a restaurant called La Gonelle, which looked out over the marina.

Emmanuèle got up.

'I can't help myself. I have to do this. You don't mind?'

Serge shrugged his shoulders. M. egged her friend on.

'Go on! Go on!'

She was already taking off her tracksuit. She asked the restaurant owner if there was somewhere she could change.

You dived into the marina as we looked on in bewilderment. We watched you weave between the hulls of the yachts amid the fuel oil and the six-packs. You came back dripping wet, ate the paltry pieces of fried cuttlefish we had left for you and the bit of chorizo that spiced it up.

*

O eyes of purer blue than the sky after the passing of the pitch-black storm cloud!

*

She had for many years been a boxer. The after-effect of a devastated childhood. At last, she had become the hitter rather than the hit. And, in a restaurant, on a train, by a swimming pool, on a plane or in the ferry taking us to the island's landing stage, the damaged little girl, the frantic boxer, would be constantly reaching for her bag and taking out a little round mirror. She was completely preoccupied with her damaged face. Ten times a day, her face is her only concern –

adjusting her hair, powdering her nose, opening her lipstick. She takes a look at herself. She sighs.

Chapter XIII

Water

On each of his paintings, when he felt it was finished, Eugène Boudin would note the day and the hour. Never the year. He would sometimes add the wind direction and speed. But he never noted the year. Something about noting the hour *but not the year* is more temporal than it would be to write nothing at all. Something eternalising. The temporal, but anti-annual – and even anti-seasonal – note that Eugène Boudin took pains to add to the bottom of his paintings turned them into non-biographical ecstasies between land and sky – ecstasies more meteorological and impersonal, the opposite of sempiternal. Contemplations of nature on its own, in the unpredictable moment, the pure moment of time, the *temporary* moment of time.

*

The enigma of the Earth – first of the sea throwing up its waves on its crust; then of life engendering itself in the depths of the abyss and rising to the peaks and crests of the mountains; lastly, of nature developing upon the lava of the volcanoes emerging from the sea as they send up their vast domes of smoke; the flowers opening, the birds ascending and soaring among the clouds, the animals moving and devouring, and we – so tiny, so numerous – devouring them, culling them, wiping them out. The key to the puzzle has been lost and perhaps even corrupted beneath cubic metres of water moved by the moon, by the polarisation of the poles, by the gravitation around the core of fire at the centre of the Earth.

*

Twice a day, the tide forms four powerful surges of water around the rocks. A sonata in four-four time, more ancient than all the forms of life that have restrained them. A downbeat of withdrawal, followed by a downbeat that sets it rising. This is the initial formula that sets the rhythm for the forming of forms.

*

A secret concealed as it 'goes to ground' under the water. Crabs hide silently beneath the seaweed, beneath the stones, beneath the clumps of mussels, among the shrimps forming their carapaces; they seem still to be walking, though they are, in fact, swimming; the seaweed comes adrift in the stagnant darkening water; seems to break free, seems to detach itself from its roots and escape. Velvet swimming crabs slip into the shade of the rocks. What, like them, feeds only on sick animals, old anemones, briny water and warm sunrays?

*

Being born, he is in the world after he existed, always behind on the original impulse. The beginning is always behind on the original impulse. In language, the present is not possible, since it has to be learnt. The foetus cannot speak. The *infans* cannot speak. Time takes its time in the body and sometimes even dies before we accede to its strange Dimension. There are people who have lived their whole lives without coming to terms with their bodies. In any event, happiness does not arrive at its appointed hour but suddenly *overtakes* the soul that feels it. It has the good fortune to outpace every kind of pace. It takes us by surprise.

*

Rage, find yourself a cause! Torrent, build the surge that will speed your thrust!

Anger, seek out an object to substitute for your desire, an object in which desire will fade away while being incorporated!

Chapter XIV

Pavia

Pigeons, though widely disparaged, have at times a simply sublime colouring on the longest remiges of their wings or on the strikingly soft down of their bellies. The colours of the constantly trembling leaves of the poplar tree. They are like veils of rain shifting over the surface of the sea and reflecting its blue tints. The cloud frays – cordage wrenched from the mast in the long rolls of seaweed ripped away on the shore.

*

Emily Dickinson in 1861: 'Say – Sea – Take me!'[x]

Rousseau says he let himself drift in his boat on the lac de Brienne. That was his goal for the day. He lay down beside the damp oars and wept out of happiness.

*

Early in 1525, during the Siege of Pavia, Francis I suddeny forgot his own self in the Italian countryside.

Not only did he eradicate his former self, but he morphed into something new. No longer did he know what he was doing: he read, he contemplated, he dreamt. It was from the depths of his dreams, then, that he invented the Loire and the chateaux lost in the forest. This genius of a king was genius enough to build what had dazzled him.

Chapter XV

The Anarythmetic

When telling someone to 'get lost', the French say 'Va voir ailleurs si j'y suis!' (Go elsewhere and see if I'm there), while the Japanese say: 'Come the day before yesterday!'

Where Japanese locates u-topia in time, French inscribes a-chronia in space.

*

'What is the rhythm of time in being?'

Vesuvius, looking out on the Tyrrhenian Sea, replies:

'79, 1139, 1631, 1944 – this is the rhythm of time in being.'

Naples was built on the slope of time that is losing its patience.

François Nomé is the real name of the painter who came from the Vosges and whom history has recorded by a finer name than the *nomen* of his origin – the extraordinary name Desiderio. Desiderio's work was, indeed, unforeseeable, stranger even than that of Elsheimer, of Caravaggio, or what was conceived by Horace Vernet, which heralded the Terror. Desiderio witnessed the eruption of Vesuvius in 1631. All his life, he remained haunted by it.

How are we to sum up his oeuvre? His oeuvre is a flaming ruin. He went on to paint only disasters. And on the seashore the silhouette of Saint Augustine and his mitre. Apart from his paintings, only a single remnant of his life has been preserved: a single written trace from his days in Naples. It is the simple note, written half in French, in the *Roll of Painters Resident in the City*: '*Monsù Desiderio pittore exerçoit à Naples l'année venue 1640*'.

He alludes to the volcano when painting the port that collapses into the sea.

It was said of Desiderio that his studio could bring out ten to fifteen ruins a year.

A never-ending gushing of ruins.

The Gushing Ruin – that is what I call 1640.

*

Books suddenly find their readers. This is true. And that may be where the mystery of the anachrony of the beings of this world resides.

At any given moment in time, a work receives its sudden audition. Bach and Mendelssohn. Froberger in Bach. A bird in Messiaen. Does the anachrony become synchronised as the centuries pass and the celestial explosion moves faster and faster in space? No. Is it increasingly de-synchronised as the sun ages? Not that either. And yet the book and the reader suddenly mesh together in silence. Telemachus plunges his hands into the sea's waters, mumbling his father's name. And we weep. Two thousand and nine hundred years after this line was sung on the shores of Turkey.

*

Telemachus touches his father by touching the water of his shipwreck.

There again, everything sinks, everything falls. Like the hands in the sea, like the child in the father, like the father in the waves.

*

The stripping-away of subjectivity in love.

The stripping-away of subjectivity in psychoanalysis.

The stripping-away of subjectivity in old age.

The stripping-away of subjectivity in listening to music.

The stripping-away of subjectivity in the contemplation of a landscape.

The stripping-away of subjectivity in the reading of novels – even more than in the reading of works of philosophy or historical annals.

*

There is also a stripping-away of subjectivity in friendship, which is by no means necessarily a form of knowledge.

Let us say that I did not know the woman I accompanied on our tireless excursions.

Our muteness, our connivance, our reserve, the wonderful bond between us always fell short of any knowledge.

*

Rare are the women who have remained entirely meteorological.

Rare are the men who are not held hostage by the metric – and, so to speak, pulsatile – time of mobile phones.

Rare are the humans whose lives are not entirely turned toward the future of their servitude, shackled by the chronophagous consequences of sexual reproduction, or simply petrified by dint of their ongoing complicity with misfortune and the cruelty that comes with misfortune's rule.

Rare are those who have left Egypt behind even in memory, in its monuments, its slavery – those who have escaped the will of the Pharaoh.

Rare are those who have freed themselves from the peals of the church bells, who have broken from the orbit of the great clock in the city centre or the town square or on the façade of the municipal theatre.

Rare are those who have abandoned the ringing of the alarm clock, as bruising to the heart as it is jarring to the brain.

Rare are those who have unplugged their houses' doorbells.

*

Too rare are the mentally ill, the melancholic, the autistic,

the little children,

the artists wholly absorbed in their art,

the anchorites sitting in the lotus position at the

entrance to their caves,
  the wonderful depressives.

Chapter XVI

Saint Teresa

She died on one of the ten days that did not exist.

The ten days that did not exist shape the mystery of the ecstasy of St. Teresa. She came from the little Roman town of Avila. Swooning in happiness. Sculpted by Bernini.

In the incomparable, semelfactive night that leads suddenly from 4 October 1582 to 15 October 1582, in the course of that strange night when the Julian calendar cedes the *counting of time* to the Gregorian, she faints. She falls forever into a swoon. She dies.

*

We should leave empty years in the chronicle of time. We should leave virgin spaces in the forests, along the barbed wire fences of the fields, on the sides of the hills, on the clifftop plateaus. Empty stretches in our task-lists as much as on the riverbanks. Deserted foreshores between the waves and the paths, the nets, the boats. In Spinoza's writings *rarus* is a word counterposed to saturation. *Rara laetitia*: rare joy.[xi] *Sed omnia praeclara tam difficilia quam rara sunt.*[xii] For all that is luminous, all that is worthy of light, is as difficult as it is rare. A word whose ecstacising (*ek-stasis*, shifting into ecstasy) at the end of the *Ethics* – once it has been coupled with a sort of dawning, with the multicoloured radiance of light – guides the work of this odd lens-maker in search of a momentary, unmistakable, unmediated, singular, almost originary joy. It was the genius of Dürer to rescue a work from its own excessiveness, from over-fullness. To lift the hand from the drawing as the key moment of art, as Apelles said. To rescue life from language, to uproot experience from symbolic completeness. To preserve existence from logorrhoea, from chatter, from the endless circulation of voices and precepts, from the pack, from the *verbum*, from padding. At the end of the ploughed field you have to leave fallow spaces, thickets of trees, copses, bushes, clumps of thistles, white beaches, sea shores, lake shores. You have to step back from the pogrom. You have to climb the highest, most inaccessible slopes of the mountains alone or in twos – no more than twos – have to climb to the most ancient solitary regions of the first men and the first plants, find the berries they favoured, the hallucinogenic mushrooms they treasured, the tiny little shrubs – plants primitive as yet – that sprang up in nature after the glaciers receded, among the pebbles the waters had rolled there, among the shiny flint nodules their hands found tempting.

*

But where are the most solitary places now? Where are the happiest places? Where in the world is one least under surveillance? Where is one the least protected, not to say free? Where is the eye of the cyclone, at the heart of violence, where can one peacefully go to ground?

The richest have inexplicably abandoned spaces where solitaries can now return and stroll in silence: the avenues of affluent neighbourhoods in summer.

The Etruscan museums in all the small towns of Italy, so cool and deserted.

The disused village churches, their hard benches left unoccupied in the shade.

The cemeteries from which all humans have decamped, for they no longer pray to their dead.

The bleak suburban gardens behind their fences, their thuja hedges, their wicker hurdles, more disconcerted than the gods themselves, whom the candles, the vigils, the processions and the singing have abandoned.

Lastly, all the dawns, the damp cobblestones of the ports, the quays slippery with fish scales in the first white light of day, the sublime, rubbish-strewn, desolate, silent, empty little alleyways running down to the sea.

*

The word 'sol-emn' refers to the day that is 'alone' (*solus*) within the 'year' (*annus*).

'In this word, *solus* and *annus* are mingled and celebrated', said Terentius Varro. This is the invention of *anniversaire* – birthday or anniversary.

The Emperor Hadrian granted permission on one day of the year, when the capture of old Jerusalem was being commemorated, for Jews to have access to the capital of their former kingdom for the duration of that day.

He ordered that the old Hebrew name 'Hierusalem' never again be pronounced by a citizen of the Empire, on pain of death.

The city would henceforth be called 'Aelia Capitolina'.

During that single, moveable feast, on a date to be set by the Prefect, in return for the payment of an ever larger sum each year, covering only the inflation of their pain and despair, and within the space of the light provided by the sun in its course on that day, these men, condemned henceforth by the Empire to wandering and humiliation, would be allowed to come and weep over the tumbledown stonework of the temple their forefathers had built long ago.

They would touch the stonework of a ruined rampart.

They would touch the lichen and the little ferns on it.

At the last ray of the sun, the gates of Aelia Capitolina would close again on their departing shadows.

Then the pious men would return to the night, to the countryside, the shores and the sea.

Or, rather, they would slot back into the marvellous 'non-temple' that the book in their belongings had turned into.

*

Moses says in the Negev: The Sabbath is a piece of Paradise granted to Adam and given to his descendants to console them for the exile into which they had been driven by the sin of the first day.

Within time the Sabbath is the joker day.

Sunday,

an extraordinary invention in time,

by which the undergirding of what-was *lingers* in space,

In a sheath of light enigmatically *upturned* in the depths of the dark origin.

This is how Nature comes before human beings.

Nature is perhaps the finest form of Time,

deeper than Language and vaster than Being.

Chapter XVII

The Master of the Return to Origins

When the end of the Ming dynasty came – this was in 1644 – tyranny, revulsion with politics, hatred of men of letters, denunciation, strict regulation and fear prevailed. They said: 'It is the end of the Ming.'

When it was the end of the Ming, the 'Master of the Return to Origins' appeared.

His name was Hong Yingming. They also called him Master Huanchu. A native of Sichuan province, he had been the disciple of Yuan Huang. When Yuan Huang died in the year 1606, Hong Yingming began to write the *Caigentan*. Putting it as simply as can be, *Caigentan* may be translated as 'Remarks on Vegetables'. Or as 'On the Proper Use of Roots in a Period of Confinement'. Or, again, as 'How to Adapt the Source to Current History'. Such is precisely Hong's argument: 'How, being determined to retire and with my master dead and gone, can I nestle into the origin as into my mother's lap?'

*

In 1644, Hong's book is the first great Chan Buddhist work.

In 1652, on 4 January, in the light of dawn, the marvellous Jacqueline Pascal – the Emily Brontë of French history – flees rue Beaubourg forever. She gets into her carriage, heading for Port-Royal des Champs.

In 1664, having escaped from French prison, Saint-Évremond leaves by the seas around Dieppe on a light vessel, never to return.

At that same moment, Jacques Esprit is writing *La Fausseté des vertus humaines*,[xiii] which he completes in 1673 at Poitiers.

It was in the year 1669 that, without warning, the bridge at Avignon collapsed into the Rhone.

*

To the sad hours we should not add sorrow that makes them hard to bear. And perhaps, if we are superstitious, pretty much avoid adding in the waiting that brings them to a standstill. We should go to the harpsichord, the piano, the violin, the viola, the shamisen or the cello and decipher a piece of music. We should go into the garden and water the quivering shrubs or the flower petals that close up at day's end, shake from them the dust built up in the hottest part of the day; we should translate a book; we should pick up an embroidery canvas and trace out in pencil on it the drawing of our choice, the dream of our desire; we should pick up a music score and whiten it, ensilence it, embellish it, add fingering. We should seek out all the subterfuges that remove the sense of wrongs done to us that we have harboured since the time we were hungry and fed from the breasts, so long and gentle, that suckled us – exactly as we fed our dreams at night with the dishes we dreamt of in the day. Even when they are sad, it is good for hours to be free of regret.

*

When the anachronistic Bach dedicated his life to the fugue (this was from 1717 onwards), he was choosing an abandoned form.

A form that had died out two centuries earlier. A form that no longer promised success. The form of the suite was only a century old: it dated from the incendiary riots of July and August in Paris, in which Blancheroche died.[xiv]

A form that Blaise Pascal was the first to hear in October 1652.

A form that seemed so archaic to the most innovative musicians of the eighteenth century that they did not compose any.

Neither Vivaldi, nor Rameau, nor Handel wrote a fugue.

Nor Mozart, nor Chopin, nor Fauré.

*

The intense sadness that emanates from such an original, pained, dark, passionate, odd book as La Rochefoucauld's fragmentary work, in the wake of the blind fury of the Day of Straws [xv] at Porte Saint-Antoine in Paris on 4 July 1652, is comparable to the sadness that leaps out from the incredibly brusque *Preludes*, which Chopin composed in the company of George Sand and her two children on the island of Majorca, with sea and storms raging. He is walking in the rain. He is spitting blood once again. He invents a strange, retrospective 'conciseness'; a sudden volte-face of sheer wildness and extraordinary pride; a nostalgic commotion containing, at the same time, an inexplicable, undiluted rage.

This is what the two of them invent with an act of fragmentation. Death is stalking the footsteps of both from one hour to the next. They are hounded by it all the more for the fact that the two women they have, both of them, loved so madly, have not been constant in their lives. This is, perhaps, the impenetrable region of the distress they are experiencing, though it has taken a fabulous turn, assumed an unforeseen course.

*

In July of 1882 at Zurich, Liszt, aged 72, plays for a stunned Fauré the *Ballade* the latter has just composed.

A Fauré quivering with emotion at the water gate beside the river Limmat.

Fauré's work that suddenly became shot through with a sharpness, with pain, love and beauty, in the aftermath of the 1914–18 war.

Chapter XVIII

The Ruins of Jumièges

She steps onto the gangway. He jumps into the rowing boat. All is adventure. There is only a departure. Even in the end, there is only a beginning. In life, in death, there is only a start, a departure.

She gets into the carriage on the cobbles of rue Beaubourg. Dawn has not yet broken.

*

In January and February 1450, King Charles VII is at Jumièges with Agnès Sorel who has settled peacefully in front of the fire at the manor house in Mesnil-sous-Jumièges, preparing for her labour. She dies in childbirth. Just before she expires, she bequeaths eight hundred gold crowns to the abbey, then requests her Book of Hours. She had time to read the 'Seven Verses of St Bernard for Escaping Damnation', then suddenly uttered a 'loud, high-pitched cry on Monday the 11th day of February in the year 1449 (the old-style year, running from Easter to Easter) at six hours past midday'. In the ruins of the abbey, the recumbent statue of the Dame de Beauté, as she was known, has disappeared, stolen at the Revolution. All that remains is the black slab, lost amid the globe thistles.

*

During their adulterous affair, the Duc de la Rochefoucauld and the Duchesse de Longueville communicated with the aid of Books of Hours of different colours, like the white and black sails of Tristan and Isolde.

The sail in the distance is white, but she says 'Black is the sail' and Tristan dies. Isolde climbs the hill, climbs the staircase in the tower, stretches out beside him on the bed and surrenders to death.

Souls, writes the duke, unravel in love 'the way rivers lose themselves in the sea.'[xvi] He almost dies at Charenton-Saint-Maurice under the maples and alders by the water's edge: there, on that 'tongue of land', he writes, 'where the rivers Marne and Seine meet'.

His passion was the passion for grand passion. It is only petty loves that absence diminishes. It increases the greatest passions, over-stimulates them. 'The way the wind blows out candles and whips up fire.' Nothing can contain the sadness or limit it. It is constantly reopening. There are only departures. Only burstings-open. The way autumn figs that have turned black burst when you try to grasp them. The way muscat grape seeds suddenly splinter and flood your teeth.

*

504 fragments of La Rochefoucauld remain on that 'tongue of land'.

107 of Heraclitus in the sanctuary of Ephesus on the shores of the Aegean, opposite the island of Samos.

*

'Childhood follows us through all the ages of life.' This is the magical opening sentence of the duke's original manuscript, dating from 1660.

Chapter XIX

The Lost House

Every house has a lost house behind it.

The annihilation of the Assyrian Empire came about so quickly that when, at each succeeding stage, Xenophon asked his troops to let loose the horses in the approaches to the former capitals, those troops would forever be examining the ruins of great cities – day after day, week after week – cities levelled to the ground and now nameless.

Shapeless waves of attrition and decay, of dust whipped up by the wind that drives the dunes, wind that disinters objects from the sand, then reburies them – all so strangely *unnameable*.

Xenophon interrogated the peasants who were still hunkered down in the erosion of a world. He questioned the poverty-stricken individuals who had suddenly taken to begging as they saw the Greek troops coming. Yet no one could tell him by what name the ruins he was pointing to had been known. These here.

Those there, pointing with his finger. Those there, with his hand. Those there, with his two arms outstretched in prayer or supplication.

Then, even language, which is the ruin of the sensory world, abandoned the memory of these demolished cities that time had piled up in these once rich regions turned to desert, beneath the dust of the stars, carelessly trodden upon by the horses of Xenophon's army.

Curiously, names, time and meaning came back to them one day. Two hundred years ago, the *tells* of broken clay bricks ceased to be cities destroyed thousands of years ago.

They became books.

*

The past is so unstable.

Who knows what the past has in store for the future?

We know nothing of what awaits us in the depths of the world from out of the depths of the world.

Time does not know what the non-homogeneous duration of night has stored up in the depths of the origin.

*

They were no longer stones lying in the sand.

It was no longer silence accumulated inside the crumbling that the sun forces on the insubstantial clay as it dries it.

These bricks trampled underfoot, crushed beneath his horses' hooves, were thousands of tablets covered with small wedge-shaped letters that sounds now returned to settle on, like butterflies on flowers. Or like birds knocking with their beaks against mounds of earth, to demolish them and get to worms, grubs, chrysalises, ladybirds, flies or caterpillars.

At that point all these collapsed towers of Babel rose again in the mirage of time.

*

Then, in the *blood* of time, all these names and letters and books and languages were one day deciphered and restored.

Gilgamesh in Ur.

Enkidu in the oases of the salt marshes.

More than that, all these things now *became a murmur* once again on the lips of scholars, epigraphists, archaeologists, historians, and guides. Everything was named. And all that was named was dated. It all came back like a flood, an unpredictable torrent, now once again successive and foundational.

It returned as a story amid what had been a mere rambling and a roaming.

Returned like the chance element in happiness.

*

This is how Xenophon's question was answered with a two thousand four hundred year delay. This is how the beginning of human fires – of the human hearths later called ports and cities – suddenly burned itself out silently, amid lethal dread, on the plains of northern Europe, in the heart of the twentieth century. Dry seasons. *Nox sine nomine.* A night with no name by which ever to be called, nor ever to be narrated.

Chapter XX

La rue du presbytère

Behind the windowpane, daylight is not yet there, but dawn has broken, its pale light enough for us to start seeing nearly everything.

I can make out the silhouette of someone running.

The beach and the sea shrouded in white mist.

You cannot see the islands.

*

Returning to the place where she was happy brings me joy. I skirt the low wall of the presbytery. Here is the site of the bottle bank, where the road forks. Next to the pond full of catfish. Here is the peg for closing up the packet of peanuts or almonds so they don't get damp. I take the secateurs from the bucket at the entrance. The vine she loved needs tending. The grapes need to be cut and placed in the salad bowl on the kitchen table. And the ripe figs gently twisted off.

The pear tree against the wall doesn't get the rain. Where is the watering can? She always left it by the hosepipe, the long, soft yellow hose she never reeled in. Why isn't it there anymore? I do not know if it's joy I'm feeling at reviving the happiness. I do some watering. There are even people who aren't happy to be happy. I love the countless golden alyssum bushes, all clumped together, so tightly crowded and downy, with so sweet, captivating a scent. But this pain, mingled with the gentle warmth of the sun – what can its name be? Why shall the pair of pheasants by the bay tree, in the garden of this house, outlive the span of time she had to watch them, marvel at them, and rejoice in them?

Chapter XXI

The Hunt

In 1860 the allied fleets took Tientsin. The French troops reached Peking by forced marches. At Haidian they ransacked the palace.

The sergeant of the Spahi cavalry corps, Hérisson by name,[xvii] wrote his mother the following letter:

> You might have thought it was an anthill, trampled underfoot by some passer-by: the panicked worker ants were fleeing in all directions with a seed, a grub, an egg or a wisp of straw between their mandibles. There were troopers from the Yonne with their heads buried in red lacquer trunks. Belleville peasants stuffed rubies, sapphires and pearls in their pockets, down their shirts, in their caps. Sappers serving in the Engineers had brought their axes and swung them to break down wardrobe doors. From time to time, someone would shout 'fire!' and everyone would run out. Then they'd all come back and go on with their

pillaging. When, after walking through all the imperial apartments being ransacked by my men, I came out in the palace grounds, the eternally tranquil spectacle of nature in this long garden sent a shiver down my spine. The trees were majestic, the pond a well of silence, the moon visible in the grey sky. Here and there – everywhere – groups of Frenchmen ran mutely to the pavilions, the pagodas, the libraries, the boats. I went and sat in an abandoned gondola and fell asleep.

*

1870, that most accursed year of all, the worst year of the nineteenth century, not excepting Waterloo or the Capture of Peking, saw the last hunt with hounds in which the Emperor of the French, Napoleon III, took part.

It was at Fontainebleau, where his great-uncle had said his farewells in 1814.

At the end of the chase, they propped up the wounded stag against a rock in the forest to afford the emperor the illusion of dispatching it.

The emperor raises his rifle, takes aim at the stag, and kills the finest dog in the pack.

*

Athenian democracy and the Weimar Republic: two droplets of light fallen into the lap of chance.

Holland after the Union of Utrecht.

Japan closed to shipping.

Chapter XXII

The Temple of Time

Narrabo omnia mirabilia. I shall tell of all the marvels, and I shall tell of them from the hiddenmost depths of the soul, in the fever of its dreaming, in the temple, *tempula*, of time. What is called a marvel (the *mirabilia*, the wonderful things) is the pure tragic eventality that leaves us stupefied (Tacitus), dazed and in tears (Sima Qian), or drunk with the ferocity of the crowd (Michelet).

The marvel is the uninterpretable detail. So closely related to the dream. For psychoanalysts, detail in a dream that has no rational explanation can be seen as signifying resurrection.

*

The mirabelle plum tree in my sister Marianne's garden, up above the village of La Turbie, above the Tropaeum Alpium, above the sea.

Its marvel – its *mirabelle* – recurs so often in my dreams.

*

In the bombed-out port of Le Havre, *merveille* was the word for the succulent doughnuts, moulded into the letters of the names of the four children, which my mother tossed into the sizzling oil the day before. The initials of tiny people, empty as yet of their worlds, that swelled miraculously in the black pan.

That bronzed in the oil until they turned golden.

They were dusted with caster sugar.

They were wrapped in a cloth so as not to dry out overnight. We unwrapped them and ate them at the breakfast table in the morning. And, on top of being marvels, they were miracles: wolfing them down, we were wolfing down ourselves.

*

Such are the dates within chronicles.

In the pyrology of the soul – behind the firebreak of the ceremonies of death, beneath the shrouds of the dead, beneath the granite slab.

Living history is linked to desire when that desire

disappears.

And, even more often, when the blood that has been shed seeps away into the ground. History merely brings the arrangement of a narrative. 'What is history?' was a question suddenly posed by the first great historian of the West, who bore the name Thucydides. *Men bring their memories into harmony with their ills.*[xviii]

The untellable can only return if we invent a jewel-box to put it in. A case to hide it in. An ark in which to keep it from prying eyes. We call this a novel.

Or, in days gone by, a crypt beneath the choir. A reliquary beneath the gold and enamel crucifix.

A nook in a room or a cell. A remote pocket where society loosens its grip. A place of retreat or respite where the narrative begins anew.

A poem by pure emotive insurrection. An unsinkable fragment.

The male sex that stands erect beneath its covering fabric. The female sex quivering in the recesses of its concealing lingerie.

The elements, for all their incongruity, slot together in the magical mistake.

In the act of love, the soul suddenly rises up with the beating of the heart. The two temples beating. For no sort of unity. Yet nostalgia for that unity rose up in full force at the height of the embrace.

*

In 1640, walkers with lanterns visited what they called 'the ends of the world': we call them caves. Niaux was visited in 1640. There they saw crude scenes, which they assumed had been drawn by wolf-children who had been left exposed to die, far from the village, as expeditiously as possible.

*

Roman coins, minted in the year 235 and dating from the reign of the Emperor Constantine, were found on the island of Okinawa, in the ruins of Japan's Katsuren Castle that was burnt down in 1242.

*

In the wake of the successive Persian, Macedonian, Christian, Muslim, British, Turkish, Japanese, German, American, Russian, Chinese, French, Cambodian, Arab and African horrors, historians, grown frightened, obsequious and scheming, so very intelligent and cowardly, gave up on the scrupulous examination of events. They gave up on Ajax, his death, his loneliness, his uncontrollable anger, his sword, his silence, the silence of his tall, beautiful wife Tecmessa, covering his body with the great shroud. They went over to Ulysses's camp, with his chatter, his cunning, his incurable nostalgia. They not only began to fear for their salaries as state functionaries; they were overwhelmed by horror at the vertiginous, purposeless, bottomless, erudite hole of Time itself, falling from the sky drop by drop, alongside the blood of Ouranos or, blast by blast, in the sporadic – and, to be frank, catastrophic – factuality of moments of distress and the inexplicable – implacable, aimless, sumptuous – contingency of dates.

They preferred to give more meaning to their books and less exposure to their lives, at the risk, in their terror, of manifesting less truth.

A loss of precision ensued. And a decrease in erudition.

Can those who set out to sail far from shore still speak of that shore once it is out of sight? Even the regret that hounds them, the yearning, the impetuous nostalgia for return have wandered off on to objects other than the one that should have been theirs, as it had been so at the sources of history. They focus now on a more immediate danger. They refuse to collude in the submersion threatening them, the submersion they fear.

Though it may be that those who remain afloat can properly speak of upstream (where they are not yet) and downstream (where they shall never again be), who in time can speak of a reference point in the depths of space or in the flow of time and its inconstant speed?

East, West, North and South, zenith and nadir do not exist in the space that spills into being.

Post, *ante*, here, not-here, *hic* and *alibi* (here and elsewhere), *fort* and *da* (gone and here) in time – these directions are not even the product of our bodies facing the rising sun, but are produced by the order that minds and ages have created with the words of language, with parts of sentences, with inflections of words, with the persons of verbs, with the *tempora* of the sequences that articulate the dialogues addressing themselves to the matter, not so as to discover such properties there, but to smuggle them in. No point where we are persists even in the moment when we undergo its effects. But even then, there is no way for them to be where they are, nor to remain where they will no longer be. All the cells present in our bodies at our birth are no longer active. No longer are they the cells which cause our blood to pulse so violently.

We are entirely empty not only of what we were, but of what we are becoming.

*

The dead interval is humans' only dwelling-place. The dwelling-place of their hunger in the day they come to know. But also the foetal period before they enter the atmospheric light. The lack within desire and, in the depths of desire, is the dream. The hole in the future that is not only death, the void vaster than death, which bears down on them like a raging torrent.

At the beginning of Book VI of his *De lingua Latina*, the scholar Varro wrote prodigiously: 'Time is a bending, a flexion, but it is also a void. In our language, the word *tempus* articulates either an *intervallum* in the movement of the world itself or a *flexio* within the words that refer to it. This is the reason why cases and flexional endings are called the *tempora* of language.'

What are *tempora* – tenses? Knees that bend, inflections in desire, inversions in joy. Heartbeats that combine with the briefest, most uneven murmurs. Sonic ebbings of the breathing of life at the end of the words relating it after that life has finished. A strange dance of revenants returning more and more into the ever-more-recent ruins of cities in a history which, for its part, grows older and older.

Thus, time is an interval between the movements of the world as it is articulated by the natural language that passes the lips and teeth of those who devour, that transcends the digestion of the predators once their hunger has been sated, that addresses itself to the ears of those who hear memories of it, the wild beasts nosing around, their hunting, the violence of the battles between prey and predators, the killings determining the survivors of an hour and the eternal victims.

An interval that passes into a growing void.

But more than this irreducible narrow passage that runs between lips and ears, the word *tempus* in Latin not only interlinks the physical world and the verbal, it refers to living life which it hunts out, and the pursuit of which inflames it day on day. It refers to the *vita viva* that is the distinguishing mark of that ancient world which remained more savage than many others at an equal level of civilisation. More *instinctual.* Time, *tempus*, connects to the temples, *tempulae*, on either side of the human face, where the internal, foetal, ante-natal, pre-atmospheric pulsing of blood signals that the body is alive, that the life harboured within it is impulsive. Not only does it indicate its emotion, but it gauges its energy, its level of excitation, its warmth, its ruddiness: things which, precisely, make up the fever born from the flow by which it is measured.

One places one's thumb on the pulse.

Chapter XXIII

The Cosy Nook for Memories of the World

At summer's end, the jelly shoes are put away, along with the swimming trunks, the white buckets for gathering shellfish, the fishing nets that the children prodded into the pools along the very edge of the foreshore, at the outer fringe of the sea's reach, the rope sandals and the straw hats. The recliners are folded away. The sunshade with its pale hues rolled up. They are all stowed away at the back of the garage.

*

We, too, when approaching death, hide ourselves in the cosy nooks of our living rooms, in the shadows, by the little tilted lamps that spare the eyes, modestly inhabiting a skin or body that age has rendered ugly or, at least, stretched and creased, in the avoidance of a morrow that begins not to figure in the calendar, in the apprehension of bad things that are, on the one hand, multiplying and, on the other, growing more distinct; bad things that one senses are coming and that one ends up watching out for. We hide in the corner of the curtains, by the window, in the company of books – that is to say, we hide in the memories of the world. We evade our fear in the liveliest memories the world has left us. We withdraw into the most affecting moments that were experienced at the tenderest and most devastating times of childhood. We take pleasure in stirring them deep within ourselves, in reliving them.

*

It is good, in the hours of daylight or in the creation of art, to find moments of sustenance in beloved memories.

And that is, in fact, how dreams operate as soon as one closes one's eyelids at night.

*

Happy the hours that break free of the social, historical or even familial, even biographical, chronicle of events. Moments no one knows of, concealed by the obscurity of private life – life so private that it wishes to be shorn of consciousness. Scenes protected by the silence of the senses and the so intimate, so inexpressible treasury of smells. Incomparable substances that belong more to the milieu than to the individual soul, much as flowers do, or at least those hardy flowers, which have mysteriously reached as far as the lawn – doubtless over the winter, doubtless following a shift in the winds, doubtless on the end of a bird's beak, their appearance enchanting us in the new spring.

*

Where are the blue tuberoses? Blue turning to grey? Aquamarine?

Happy hours, where are you?

*

Where is the wall?
    Where is the house?
    Where is the port?

Chapter XXIV

General History

If time, strictly speaking, is defined by the delay in the passage of light – from the Sun to the Earth – light illuminating its own path after travelling it, that remarkably mysterious lapse of time hollowed out of space and fading there, that self-erasing fold, that strange stretch of time, accentuated, with increasing mystery, more by the thrust carrying it onward than by the impulsion that initiated it, it is also because this point of time's distension is its only referent, not the moment in which the 'now' might occur. Time is what is irrecoverable in this delay.

It is this waiting vis-à-vis the delay.

It is thus, too, that the blind point of language is the only reflection, and nothing is mirrored in it.

What irradiates, once was.

A music makes their hearts, and beats in the universe with just a two-beat rhythm.

Therein lies the origin of the division into the two

sexes when life advanced.

There is something of darkest night in the background to the frenzied, incommensurable light of the stars which hurtle on in space toward their missing mass.

The hallucinatory, historic point that moves with humans has no temporal source. Nor does it have an end that can pass for being alive. The cosmos is not alive. Nor is the night.

Only nature lives.

Life on this Earth devours this delay from the light-giving star. The whole of its vegetation rises toward the light, gnawing away at it the moment it reaches its corollas, its crowns, its heads, its lips.

Life on Earth has never been lit by a sun whose rays were themselves *contemporaneous* with the sight they made possible.

*

The explosive character of the Hiroshima and Nagasaki bombs was wrenched from the *stellar source of the universe*, a source from which human beings were derived in the course of an *immensely* extended, millennia-long explosion.

*

In a blue and yellow tapestry, we see King Louis XI holding in his hand the 'horologe monstrable'.

The fingers of the mistrustful, scholarly, wily King Louis are holding the *horologe* like a little lantern.

It was in the late fifteenth century that the word *monstrances* came into use in French for watches.

The great lords hung their portable *horologes* (their *heures montrables* or showable hours) on the flaps of their clothes, in the form of purses to be unlaced or eggs to be half-opened.

Then, in the course of the seventeenth century, *eggs* gave way to *onions*. I do not know the reason for these highly strange names they were given, when resemblance to other objects would have served just as strangely.

Following the French Great Terror, these *monstrances* were fixed onto bracelets above the hand, around the wrists, preceding the signet rings that left their impressions on the wax which sealed the letters that went off by post. The hours were worn like ships' prows, just after the servile rings of marriage.

*

The first large-scale military order for 'wrist watches' was placed by the German Navy's General Staff with the Swiss watchmaker Girard-Perregaux at La Chaux-de-Fonds in 1881.

*

All chronometry produces origin.

Every point placed in time creates an Advent, and instantly suggests a time preceding the reference date of which the time being measured is a part. Since it cannot enter into what is being counted, the Advent of Being does not exist. And yet it 'exists'. It is even the proper meaning of the verb *ek-sister*, which signifies neither being nor living. The metric time that chops up the activities of human beings is a chimerical 'upstream' production. And not only does measured time invent this non-existent precession as a way of ordering what succeeds it (which in reality does not succeed, since the origin is continually beginning), but the primal scene does the same with our bodies in the depths of the dreams that we form around it. Coitus, the remnant of which is each of our bodies – each body in which we no longer perceive it – itself becomes imaginary in the dreams manifesting our desires, dreams in which their emotional, phantasmatic, oneiric, legendary filiations are grounded. For a sexed individual, the fact of existing conjures up that scene in which the one imagining it was not present; he hallucinates sexes which are not only not his own, but are charged with having conceived him before he appeared in Being. His 'existence', his motricity, his tact and his e-motion generate this 'upstream' during which these two earlier sexes are distorted and locked together for a moment – a lapse (*lapsus*) of time – in order to conceive *him*. Thus the word in the Bible denoting the Fall – *lapsus* – is no different from that for a lapse of time. Thus every birth forces upon the animation of the mind, *anima*, the impossible sight of the scene of its conception, without contemporaneity with such a scene ever being possible.

*

The musician, the autist, the scholar, the madman, the melancholic, the theoretician, the contemplative are not aimless errors: they are 'existentials'.

Upstream from the explosion, they have kept their footing in the very heart of the implosion.

*

Past and future are merely morning and evening between sky and Earth.

Are merely dreams in the night when consciousness collapses.

If we view the present from the standpoint of memory, we call it past.

If we view the past from the standpoint of the future, we call it dead.

If we view the Erstwhile from the standpoint of the past, we call it future, and the potential of what was pours out in a surprising way – at once non-destinal, unoriented, disordered and inexhaustible. It is what is called *pulsio*, thrust, *phusis*. So it is that the mirror neither conceals anything nor sees. What it chiefly does is reverse everything on the surface of the space that it offers up to space. That is why the inverted point of view is the only right one for reversing the reflection once again. This is what the eye does that has no mind or soul: in the depths of its vision, it simply reflects its reflecting. It is what, long before philosophy, Heraclitus called 'palintropy', which he made the core of his thinking: his inverted war. He restores to its proper place what was the wrong way about. This is what all animals do when confronted with other animals. They never look at themselves: they fear for *their* skins in the gaze of the others.

*

In his dining room Goya painted, *a fresca* and over the entire facing wall, Chronos taking a child in both hands and devouring him, the child screaming in pain as the God's jaws tear the raw, naked figure apart.

Chapter XXV

Skates and Rays

Tellus is the Earth goddess who stays beneath the sea. I watched her standing against the bay window of the kitchen. I watched her consulting – contemplating – the tide tables, calculating the width of the beach, the depths that would need to be traversed, the currents that would need to be crossed and their strength, the opposition of sun and moon, the violence of the wind, the gusts that had been forecast, and the momentum she would generate when swimming.

She was telluric. She was the *tellus*, the substratum that lies beneath the soil in which nature is rooted. The foundation of the world. That thing so fine in yoga's ascetic discipline: its foundational position. The wonderful upright posture. Only by that pose is the Buddha so handsome. Dancers were originally swimmers. The Sirens, clinging on by their claws, with their low, open shoulders, their pert breasts, their straight backs, their heads held naturally upright on the rocks out at sea. A plumbline of beauty. The goddess Amphitrite centred in the light, centred in the internal and external light, supported by the reflection of her body on the glass pane, facing the narrow palm tree, the fig tree laden with fruit down below on the grass. Then facing the seaweed and the sea anemone. This is how they say Amphitrite seduced Poseidon at the Pillars of Hercules. Dance is a memory of swimming extending into atmospheric space and reaching for the sky. That swimming takes its leave of the Earth. It then becomes the slow, slow flight of the tiny barn owls with their enormous wings in the silence of the night: it is the sublime fins of the manta rays that move – or, rather, manoeuvre – in the unlit night of the ocean depths.

*

Not finding a footing and not losing one's footing in this 'out of one's depth' situation.

Flying derived from swimming.

*

Oeufs de raie – the so-called 'mermaids' purses' with their skates' eggs – on the scorching sand, at the foreshore's edge: little black sacs with four filaments like arms and legs, resembling the image of the human body in the first drawings small children make. The body is first experienced as a closed cell. Then, in small children's - hasty rather than tentative - hands, it comes to be spontaneously represented as a sac with four linear extensions.

*

Far, far off, entering the immense waters of the sea is a tiny, clearly delineated, semi-naked body penetrating another - immense, formless, intangible, ungraspable - body that pits its resistance, its density and its sizeable force against it.

The entire personal form of the body is under attack; the whole of the flesh of the woman penetrating the gigantic volume of water is there, intensely present, lent precision by the cold, sounded out by the sea, plumbed to the depths of its life.

In sexual pleasure, particularly at the moment of climax, the image of the body is no more than a dot.

You need to go into the sea to feel your toes one by one as they sink into the sand the seaweed, the wrack or the silt, your ankle as it gets into the waves, your calves, your thighs, the fold between thigh and belly, your sex, your buttocks, your navel, your nipples that harden, your lips, cheeks and hair – right to the top of your shell of a skull. You are all aquiver. Your whole body comes into contact with water that is older than yourself, void of all form, wild, turbulent, dimensionless, chaotic.

*

A dog or a child howls as they enter the sea. It's a war. It's a conflict of forces and yelps and splashes in the waves which hit them and from which they recoil – though even as they recoil, they go forward. Like the waves, which seem to be retreating as they advance. All is howling. Trampling, assault, dishevelment, whirlwind or dance: all is howling. The dance or aspiration of the wild thrust confronting, and joining with, the physical thrust of the world.

*

The force the ocean pits against the body that penetrates it, the movement that advances constantly toward the fleshly form which itself desires that violence – this pressure, which the original water exerts and which sculpts the body, this *impression* of the original water that persists forever in the body it has shaped – is present again even more unfinished, even more *infinite* in the chaos and din that the waves make at the foot of the rocks or on the shore.

*

'I'm not swimming. It seems to me I'm sinking', Claude Faïn told me in a dream during which life and death seemed to me to be infinite 'pressings-forward'.

Claude Faïn was at Édith Dahan's in 1969. I had been struck by this confidential remark. It returned in the form of a dream. I tell myself it's probably a false memory. Even these names, which reappeared distinctly in the dream, are themselves uncertain. I am at Édith Dahan's. A very beautiful flat. It is the late sixties. I am with Paul Celan. *L'Être du balbutiement* had been out for some months.[xix] Claude Faïn explains to me what psychoanalysis is. He loves to swim. He pitches himself into the water and swims straight ahead until he is exhausted. Then he turns over and floats on his back. That's the secret he tells me. It is not about getting somewhere – to a shore, or to Ithaca, or to death. You either sink or float. You float on your back like a bit of flotsam. Death is not a headland. Void beneath it, void above. If you return, you do so in fine fettle.

*

Icarus's tomb was pointed out on a headland in the Aegean Sea, in the Amber islands.

Chapter XXVI

Elvers

When elvers reach old age, when they at last arrive from the Sargasso Sea, when they try to swim back up the estuaries, when they come seeking the freshwater of the rivers and settle onto the sand of their banks, they shake. O how those delicious elvers shake! They are just a few centimetres long and very pale, almost translucent. You point an electric torch at their weakened, dying eyes and they rush toward it to die. You wash them in water with a dash of vinegar. You prepare a court-bouillon with a carrot and a turnip and let it boil for a long time. At the last moment, you add the old dazzled elvers, covering them with white wine. You let them simmer for five minutes, then wolf them down.

*

Mer, *âme*, *See*, *Seele*: Sea and Soul.

Heraclitus said: 'It is death to souls to become water.'

And it is their origin.

Water is as ungraspable as darkness is untouchable. It is just as irresistible, as fusional, as unobjectifiable, as shapeless.

On the long, nine-month darkness that patiently bides its time in the depths of women's wombs.

On the reasons for the melancholy of seashores. A hapless joy, as Dowland said. 'O thus my hapless joy!' dates from 1604: O thou, my *joyless joy*!

Mon heur malheureux: my unhappy happiness.

*

La Rochefoucauld: Love animates our days. The sea is the living image of everything.[xx]

*

Caspar David Friedrich's 'The Monk by the Sea' dates from 1808. The wide waters of the sea are void of any form by which to distinguish them. Time itself stretches out shapeless in the deafening, endless return of the waves, which inescapably invades the resonant cavity of the skull of the one who approaches them.

It is the vanishing of any future in the absence of an object: it is the mother rediscovered in the form of the sea.

*

The sea may be called the river of the 'selfsame', the river into which all rivers spill, in which they lose themselves. Rivers, by contrast, which have a direction, which flow downstream, are never the same, are never the sea – though they do merge with it – since, in that passing, which knows only its thrust and its flow, they never pass twice.

The movement of an endless loss.

So it is with the Kaystros at Ephesus.[xxi]

*

What is water if not our ancestor? At the tips of our fingers are those remnants of fish scales that we see all the time without seeing them. When we take, when we hold, when we touch, when we play.

*

At times we go wrong without noticing it. We do not

even know where the error began. Driving fast down the motorway, you suddenly see a name and mistake it for another. You put your foot down, take a wrong exit and find yourself in some unknown place. Before you lies a crossroads with any number of streets branching off, none of whose names mean anything to you. You drive round in circles, unable to get back on the motorway that you left on an impulse, or because a name glimpsed on a road-sign struck a chord, or from some residual memory or other delusion.

Suddenly you can't get to a place that's so close but isn't showing up on the signs anymore either on the minor road, or the motorway, or at the many exits of the roundabout that you keep circling dizzyingly, but to no avail.

The nearest of things has become so very far away.

This is how I see unhappy love.

*

The French word *déboire*, which now means a setback, originally referred to the aftertaste left in the mouth by a wonderful wine you had drunk hours earlier.

*

François de la Rochefoucauld: 'Some people cannot bear to have the deep recesses of their hearts probed.'

*

In 1936, Freud replied curtly to Binswanger: 'I have always lived on the ground floor or even in the basement of the building – you maintain that on changing one's viewpoint one also sees an upper floor, housing such distinguished guests as religion, art, and philosophy. You are not alone; most cultivated specimens of *homo natura* think likewise. It just so happens that I cannot think the way you do.'[xxii]

The low-down hypothesis is the only illuminating one – simply because that is how light itself tracks in space – downwards.

And it is the only one that arrives right on time.

Or almost so, since there is always an interval within the mind perceiving it.

An interval of a sort of pain or error.

We live in a world where light and heat take some improbable minutes to reach us from the sun.

*

In the recurring dreams that I have in the depths of

night, I am readying myself to arrange a journey to such distant regions that there are no maps for it. At the crossroads of the dream or, rather, the forks in the path, the direction of travel cannot be determined. The problem I face is a simple one: I do not know how to go about reserving a seat that does, however, happen to be empty.

I no longer know how to go about booking a room, a seat or a table.

One day, without any warning or premonitory hint, you entered an enigmatic region.

The worst thing is that this landscape also has its magic.

And there is nothing to disabuse us of our bewitchment because it hasn't really deceived us. Doubtless, it is murky. It is incoherent, certainly. It is full of misleading flashes of insight. It is surprising, yet at the same time beautiful. You do not know what name to give it. You do not know how you got there.

*

One knew nothing of an error that one did not, in all conscience, even commit.

In China, a man living near a clay pit in the forests of Henan suddenly and without realising it, became a yellow and black swallowtail butterfly. He no longer knew how to sort out in his mind the various reigns, how to tell waking from sleeping, to identify mirages, echoes, the corollas of flowers or the insects that suck at them and the dreams they have.

*

One day I entered a darkened stage with a raptor on my arm, as Baisao[xxiii] was selling tea in the shadow of the bamboo trees.

I was, myself, caught off guard. It was like a dream scene I was entering, without knowing exactly how to enter, nor where to put my feet, nor how to control them. A scene in total darkness behind the theatre's house curtain.

It was there, in the old Consistory of the Chartreuse Saint-Jean, that I improvised the *Parcours labyrinthique*.

Giving an unpredictable form to one's own life and holding to it whatever it might become: such is the aim of *askesis*.

Inside the puzzle, each person then becomes that mark of luck appearing simply to have fallen from the sky.

Bon heur. Happiness, good fortune – a stroke of luck.

Mal heur. Unhappiness, bad fortune – an ill-starred fate.

The star under which birth occurred: the interval from the origin, whose influence it garners. Gradually, what once was comes to belong to him as his own niche; he nestles into it; he fuses with it.

Like an embryo in the dark, distant, forever invisible sac; like a little mulberry buried deep in the mysterious inner pouch of its mother. Hanging from its wall of skin.

This is how one *saves one's skin* in the world around one.

*

The first person I admired was a ferryman on the riverbank.

The second went into the forest to make bundles of firewood.

The third sold hot tea in a bowl.

The fourth wove straw sandals.

The fifth pulled on strings above the pelt of a cat that he had scraped and stretched out on a wicker frame: it emitted a deeply moving, regretful sound.

The sixth patiently arranged flowers in an old earthenware pot which he placed in front of the face of a stone, down which he trickled water each day.

This is how the ancient sages departed this world, slipping away through some sort of fissure.

One day in 1735, on Japan's main island, the monk Baisao turned into the steam floating on the surface of the tea he had been boiling.

*

One day in 1644 on the island called Great Britain, Izaak Walton chose angling. Just sitting on the riverbank with his rod was enough for him. These things are described as occupations, rituals, acts of contemplation. They are, in reality, wondrous disappearances.

*

The monk Yoshida Kenko did not write *The Idle Hours* in 1330, as his French translators from the Japanese claim.[xxiv]

The actual title in Japanese is *The Hours without Time.*

Hours *beyond* time *within* time.

This is what Jean de France, Duc de Berry called a book of hours.

Each date becomes a focus for coincidences which, if you examine them, turn out to be stupendous.

*

One day in 2017, while I was waiting on a little wild beach on the edge of the Gulf of Saint Florent for Emmanuèle who was swimming across the bay, I saw a static group of cows. They were all of them wheeling round like the hands of a clock, trying each in turn to find some cover under a single, somewhat bare tree. One after the other they poked their muzzles for a brief moment into the cool, shaded patch that the old Corsican tree cast on the ground.

Chapter XXVII

1955–2017

When chance, absence, the night or this book cause me to think of Emmanuèle Bernheim, my head fills with light.

So seldom is there friendship between a man and a woman without any element of sex cropping up or casting its shadow.

My body rises from the depth of my body. Got to get out. Off to the sea. Or at least to the paths that lead to the sea. I can hear her puffing and blowing in front of me, taking great, long, extremely determined strides. The understanding between us has always been absolute and resolutely unspoken. Though writers, we never talked about literature. Films were made from our books but we never talked about cinema. The people we lived with were born in the same country, one in the port of Sousse, the other in the port of Tunis, but we never spoke of our respective lives. Never. And we never talked politics.

With two exceptions: family madness, and *amours diaboliques*. First, our atrocious childhoods, the abuse, then the renewed violence. We were two damaged children. One was pushed to the point of anorexia in the days after his birth and driven to eating in the dark, the other to the point of bulimia as soon as she grew to womanhood. We had both spent our difficult childhoods in little Normandy villages. We were both little disoriented Normans, full of mud, vegetable soup, swallowed or lost words, tart apples and constant rain. She from Elbeuf, I from Verneuil. From the very first day, she took me for a psychoanalyst. We lunched at the bar of the Hotel Pont-Royal. I remember I began by suggesting that she leave Denoël, which had just brought out her first book, and I offered to publish her next book at Gallimard. But she told me her entire life story, poured it all out like a grain wagon into the unloading bay – a story mingled with disappointments, disdains, horrors, and tall stories too – with despair so difficult to confess that they left her suddenly speechless. The other exception was scatology: while I detest this restitutive aspect of the world, she always believed I had a predilection for it, for the filth, the rubbish, the provocative, exhibitionistic pile of manure left out in front of the farm as a show of wealth, by which to cock a snook at the rest of the village. She always took me for a hard-line Catholic too, because as a child at school she would be put in an empty room on her own, away from the other children, when it was catechism hour. She felt it unfair, no doubt, but above all *mysterious*. What was this 'hour', this unique 'hour' in the whole of the week, of which the Jews of Seine-Maritime were meant to know nothing? What liturgy or sorcery was hidden there? What magical practice was she not entitled to know?

*

She was Rouen and I was Le Havre. She was always charging towards the sea, in much the way the Seine winds around to do that at Rouen, then at the port of Jumièges, crossing the marshes. She always walked out in front. She walked out in front among the rocks and the great pink blocks of quartz or the big black granite boulders. She walked out in front on the paths and among the oat grasses that ran down from the hills. She speeded up when coming to the dusty coastal path that gave a foretaste of the sandy beach. And stripped off as fast as she could, removed her contact lenses, closed the little box that kept them safe, passed me her bag. She always kept her jelly shoes on her feet for swimming.

Suddenly straightening her back, suddenly moving slowly, suddenly cautious, she put on her bathing cap, tugging at the rubber of the cap, then pressing down firmly on it to drive out the air. Slipping the hair that still protruded back in, curl by curl, meticulously, though she was not meticulous. Applying the palms of her hands to her ears to ensure that this rubber afterbirth, to which she had entrusted her skull, was watertight. Despite her death, this scene recurs endlessly in my dreams.

*

In fact this scene, like any dream, anticipates the moment that comes after: the moment when she spreads her arms, raises them and brings them together again, extends them forward and dives into the sea.

*

It is Butes who one day suddenly flouts his allotted rank among the swimmers, under the stupefied gaze of Orpheus, their leader, and Jason, the captain who had the extraordinary idea for the first ship in human history. All of a sudden, with one foot on the rail of the *Argo* and not the least thought for the Golden

Fleece or for any particular destination, he dives.

*

In the swimming pool of the Hotel de Tozeur, when she sprang from the diving board to the bottom of the pool, she was an East German Olympic champion.

In the Atlantic, she awaits the surging of the tallest wave and then, head down, launches herself and bursts through it.

Personally, I am just looking at the sea and nothing more.

I am looking at the sea. At immensity. The immense force of origins.

Joy. Wave. Tide. *Wogue. Wellen.* Storm.

She was a pure bristling of waves. Pure anger!

Chapter XXVIII

Anger

After her death I quickly slipped away, as the woman being talked about was not the one I had known. I might even say I was dismayed. I had not been my friend's friend. For she was a piece of pure anguish, my friend, and that pure piece of despair, as pure as crystal, as dark as obsidian, was not there. Perhaps, out of a sense of modesty, she had not always been there with those she had loved. Perhaps too, in supporting her in her distress, I had got things wrong and merely penetrated the darkness of my own cloud. Or perhaps it was only her pain that she had sent in my direction.

*

A volcano spurting out its lava, billowing out its smoke, suddenly, unexpectedly.

The most exasperated, phobic, violent, virulent, hissing woman I have ever seen.

Pure expiration.

Pfu! Pfu!

These were great strokes of the bow that I do not know how to render without employing onomatopoeia, without breathing sounds, without dyspnoea, without a sense of stifling.

Strings that suddenly relax, sending the violin pegs awry.

Since she had been abused, she mistreated herself without counting the cost. To the point of trying to escape the very core of herself, she would charge into the headwind, into the wave about to crash into her flesh, to tire out her body, to kill herself, to huddle up against it. She would hurl herself into the water to soothe the incredible force of panic she always had inside her.

*

Bubbelee comes to mind – the little barn owl I saw being born in the Théâtre du Tinel at the Chartreuse,[xxv] a monastery dedicated to Saint John, while I was performing *La Rive dans le noir*; the little barn owl emerging from its egg – who would watch me in the darkness. I made strange little piercing pseu-pseu-pseu sounds to call him to me in the dark.

So as to hold out to him little raw, bloody bits of chicken, mouse or rat, morsels that shone a little in the darkness.

Emmanuèle, my friend, made expulsive, panicky pfu-pfu-pfu sounds in the cold air.

How I miss those little sounds – hers and mine!

*

Whose places had I entered in all those houses where I had slept? In those immense residences where I had wandered round in the dark because Hypnos, the god with great dark wings, does not want me to spend a long time in sleep each night, even though it is a state into which I collapse so swiftly? And because Nyx does not want me to escape night's clutches? It is possible that her father Chaos, the first of the gods, does not want me to wander from his disorder into the arms of his daughter. Eros does not want me to distance myself from his urgings. From his dawn.

Who did I breakfast with when all the others were asleep, the two of us up and about, silently watching the rabbits leaping on the lawn even before the early whiteness of dawn, observing the pheasants around the bottom of the branches in their fog, trying to make out the buzzard drying out its great wings up in the crown of the oak in a kind of mist that the sun would later gild.

I spent so much silent time with her.

She spent so much silent time with me.

Friendship is also knowing how to share silence, and, in that respect, we had been tremendous friends. Friendship also means never trying to tame anything in the other.

Never trying to tease out the other's deepest secret.

Letting the wildness of the other exist, the scatology, the nastiest swearwords, the panics, the body scarred with still visible traces of the blows received with such astonishment at an early age.

Let the other's madness remain. The exhalation that is beyond all sighs. Do not stimulate their *virus*, so as not to amplify their virulence.

And, above all, do not protect them from it.

Like those raptors you should never ever look straight in the face, since they will come for your eyes.

It is your eyes they devour first, before sucking on the flesh of dreams and the brain. It is with a suddenness that they alight on the gauntlet. You sense their sudden presence by their weight. Without turning your eyes toward them, you hold out a small mouse, which writhes around likewise in fear and in pain.

*

M. and Emmanuèle loved each other. Our feelings are not changed by death. The two spent hours laughing till they cried. Riotous laughter that was, without a shadow of a doubt, mingled with an underlying anxiety in them both. The two powerful women were two tormented souls. They were embers in which the same spark, the same flame passed from each to the other. One sparkled with the blue gleam of sapphires. The other threw up spurts of black flame such as you see rising from Vesuvius. They were four fiery eyes staggering back beneath the stars from the 'San Francisco', going along the little harbour, more of a marina than a fishing port, staying on the right bank, with its smell of seaweed, taking a shortcut with the blue or rusty-hued hydrangeas – enormous, full-bodied, Breton ones – and the ample wisteria mixed in among the rushes, and the great convolvulus spilling out onto the path.

They would be arm in arm, drunkenly howling with laughter.

The two of them formed a self-generating cloud of happiness that lifted itself – lifted themselves – higher and higher.

Deep in my memory, in train carriages, in airline

cabins, in 4x4s in the desert, even when face-to-face, they sent each other emails and texts, photos of cats and dogs, of stars and ridiculous talent-show judges. Short videos that doubled them up with laughter.

To speak only of journeys together.

But the only genuine way of moving in space is walking.

We could walk for hours without a word when, completely out of the blue, she would turn to you frantic, suddenly possessed and sniff very loudly. That needed translating. It meant 'Just smell that!' Or she'd stop and spread her arms lustily. That meant she was happy.

Or again, pointing at something with her chin, she'd set off towards it at an enormous lick. Translation: 'How beautiful!'

*

I reach over her towel. She sits down heavily by me. She extricates her – now bare – skull from her rubber bathing cap; ruffles what little hair she has and darts her eyes into mine. They are as blue as the eyes of Kabyle women. Or as blue as the Italian sky above the Parco Vergiliano in Naples.

Or as blue as the Tyrrhenian Sea at Capri, where Butes dived in.

The blue grotto of the Emperor Tiberius.

She darts a deep, ecstatic, half-mad glance at me and says with great – positively Churchillian – conviction: 'You wouldn't believe how good the water is!'

*

She stands there every morning in the long kitchen of the house on rue de l'ancien presbytère, her back arched, totally silent, extraordinarily concentrated, serious as a pope (Pope Innocent VI in his capella at Villeneuve), serious as a cat approaching its bowl (Boubi the chartreux, his fur faded with age), consulting the tide tables for the coves around the île aux Moines.

I am watching the tousled strands of mist as it lifts from the branches of the fig tree in the garden. The peacocks are running about and the rabbits going to ground, while within my friend – in the depths of her vigorous body – the hours and locations are silently, spontaneously being planned out. The forced marches over the course of the day: to the creeks, to the slipways, to the beaches.

You could read the whole thing on her serious face, the way the whole of a day reveals itself in the clouds of an Upper Normandy sky and disappoints.

The places we would rush off to, always depending

on the tides, were also determined by pursuit of the sun. For my part, more affected by the way the wind blew, I would crouch down like a bush on a hillside. I was suddenly like a solidly rooted clump of broom resisting the gusts. Or, like a cat, I would seek out a patch of sunlight on a bank still damp from the dew of dawn or from the now receded tide. Or I would sit straight down on the dried, cracked mud of day's end – mud still pink from the touch of twilight now flooding it with its gentle warmth. Sometimes, where the grass had been soaked by a downpour or among the fragrant brown seaweed, I would pick out some rock or other and plant myself on it, a spot where I would not get my backside soaked or frozen.

I would sometimes wait for hours.

I liked to fall into the void of time that succumbs to its own drift. True time has no direction to it. A dead end, a disappearing path. A foundational disorientation in the heart of the landscape. I liked to give myself over completely to the hypnotic din of the sea. What passivity, since my birth, has settled right into me, without my ever wearying of it?

I was not putting up with anything, nor being patient or bored. I was contemplating. Meditating. Breathing from my feet to my nostrils, right up to my forehead.

I would examine my feet, my toes in the sand as they kicked it up.

I would watch a sea anemone shrinking and fading to the point where it became something like a dry lip of vexation.

I would watch a dead starfish, sublime as a shrivelling sun.

I would watch the webbed feet of the herring gulls or the red ankle-boots of the black-headed gulls, noisily crushing the cockles, the clams and the razor-shells.

*

Little ranunculi, so wonderfully clean and white at the sand's edge.

The curlew eating his shore crab.

I held out my hand. I reached with thumb and forefinger for the little hollow tube of the samphire, crushing its corymbs to smell the heady whiff of the sea and, best of all, the delicious aniseed fragrance.

*

Beneath Emmanuèle's bag, the turnstones would lift the debris with their grasping claws and eat the little blackflies.

*

At dusk, because she still needed a swim when everyone else was going back along the paths, she would charge off into the fading sunlight. She paid no heed to the bathers who were going back down towards the harbour, who were rushing, jabbering as they went, to get the boat back to the mainland, to their hotels, their caravans, their campsites, hastening back to the world.

No heed to the blackberries.

No heed to the blue, bloom-covered sloes on the wild blackthorn bushes.

No heed to the enormous corymbs or little 'umbrellas' of the enormous elderberry bushes, to the high hollyhocks studding the island that were at least six feet tall and waving around in the evening breeze. She would blow like the mighty bellows with triangular leather straps that you see in a blacksmith's forge in the Ardennes. She would expel the air and the wind through her nose. Then, after doing so, she would summon all her strength and, jutting out her lips, thrust them away with her mouth.

*

Then, as I rounded the rock, there she was.

At the moment of densest twilight, the horizon glittered so brightly in the sun that one could not make it out.

The gilded surface burned one's eyes. I had fallen behind among the brambles and arrived after her. In the distance she was taking off her T-shirt, extracting herself from the legs of her trousers, putting on her swimsuit. How small she was. How small were humans beside the immensity of the sea. How small we were! How immense the ocean! And how it sparkled. So long and circular beneath our impotent gaze, so immense across the crust of the earth. And that immensity gradually emptied us of ourselves. It was that immensity that extended into us beneath the powerlessness of our arms. It was that immensity that was in itself attractive. It was that immensity that was the draw for all that sea water we still had in us.

Chapter XXIX

Hero's Tower

There was a ruined lighthouse at the entrance to the Gulf of Saint Florent, or perhaps a ruined watchtower for looking out to sea, that enabled Emmanuèle to judge her position as she swam across the stretch of water. It was Hero's Tower on the Bosphorus. I would go and sit some way beyond that ruined lighthouse because it smelt so foully of stale urine, filth, vomit and hot walls: a sort of wretched humanity. Emmanuèle had entirely disappeared in the sparkling bay.

Museum: how strange the word for a writer.

Hero: how strange the name for a woman in love with a man who swims over to meet her each night, crossing the strait, risking exhaustion with all that entails, going against the prevailing current, under threat of death there, or perhaps intending to die.

*

Emmanuèle, you should have chosen to die by drowning in that bay.

*

Like Marlowe's Leander, like Lord Byron when he came to Sestos, you would take off your clothes, raise your arms in the night, and dive in. You would die at the foot of the tower.

Chapter XXX

Bern

I had promised to go with her to Bern to stay with some wonderful friends. Delphine de Candolle had introduced me to them when we had travelled there by way of Lausanne and Fribourg. Emmanuèle wished to see the last country her father had known when she had helped him prepare for death. She did not want to go with family members but, at the same time, did not want to go there on her own.

*

Bern. Heim.

Everything in our lives is terribly simple.

*

We were not able to do it. The last thing she said to me – in the room at the hospital, when I was talking about our never-ending walks around the Corsican coast – after suddenly taking my hand, was: 'Oh that, yes, I'll regret we didn't do it!'

That line was so fervent and so strange, as though she were about to enter a world where regret might exist.

While she had planned her chemical death, her self-destruction, as she had done for her father, there would nevertheless have been a land of regret. A bitter sky. A sea of sighs.

I was overcome with emotion. In a previous life I must have been a stag or a hare. I have always been able to run off at great speed. I leaned over, took her leg in my hands, kissed the bare knee that stuck out from under the sheet and rushed out of the room.

I left her to an interminable ceremony. The chemicals had rendered her listless to the point where she was barely herself. The care she received was attentive, faultless. The crowd of acquaintances summoned to her bedside were no protection from death but they made the hours drag. The infusions and substances lessening her pain robbed her of the ability to manage it.

Wrenched from her own self, it was as though she was wholly at its mercy.

As I saw her like this, divested of her anger, to me she was gone.

Was she a good swimmer? No. She swam vigorously, powerfully, ferociously. She swam with an originary anguish. She was a walrus in the Barents Sea, in the heart of the winter of time and at the centre of the world. She was panting terribly when she came back and I handed her her towel. Her mouth was a nozzle. She did not so much wipe as rub herself down, as though she had the body not of a woman but a racehorse. She was still panting as she re-did her make-up, mussed up her hair, put her lenses back in, applied her eyeliner and pink lipstick and stood up again at last, still breathing heavily.

'Shall we go?'

She was already charging forward. She was already dashing off in the very essence of haste.

Chapter XXXI

November

I hate November. November is drab, rotting, heavy, slippery, almost blind. It isn't dark, it's dismal. It fills you with gloom. It's as gloomy, grey and smeary as rooks' beaks. As grim as their cawing in the ploughed fields. There are no words vile enough for November. Each year I suffer a November depression, the same way the garden suffers a November depression and the sun suffers a November depression in that quagmire of half-light and heavy cloud, that interminable slobber of mist and downpours on riverbanks, those shards of ice and strips of brown snow dangling from the shrubs, the canopies, the gutters, the alder trees. And do not get me started on subjects as sad as the year's end: those low skies, that dingy, shapeless, coagulating contraction, that stubborn cold, that dampness, those aching bones, hands no longer able to slide along the fingerboard of the cello, hands that struggle even to hold the bow or the bag handle, the ebbing of sap everywhere and the loss of flowers, that withering, that etiolation of the foliage, death of the branches, all that shade at their feet, that thickening-out, those dark leaves, that death, the falling rain. Everything falls. Everything has fallen. Nothing more to be expected of the year except the year's dying in the night. It's over.

*

Though it represents winter in daylight, the miniature in the *Livre d'heures du duc de Berry* seems like a depiction of night.

In the dark forest, a peasant is throwing his stick into the branches of the oak trees to shake out acorns.

Twenty grunting black pigs, still half-way wild boars, rush forward to rootle around for the acorns and wolf them down.

Far off in the distance, in the clearing, hunters go in for the kill.

One raises his hunting horn, as yellow as the sun.

The stag has been brought down and is held there by six dogs.

All is dark beneath the trees. Even the tops of the tree trunks are black where they meet the canopy of foliage. The sky is dark blue.

*

The sea isn't blue. The shapeless, colourless sea reflects all shapes and colours.

It turns azure only when it reflects the blue of the atmospheric cloak thrown around Earth, protecting it from the void of space.

By night, it reflects its blackness, its sublime profundity, the twinkling of the stars.

If there is a music that is God's, then the sea is God's music.

The sound it voices is as varied as its colour. Its clamorous clamour is as unpredictable as the sky itself and its squalls can be.

The sea is formless like the clouds, which are constantly changing, mutating, reflecting onto it.

The sea is even more formless than the primal world, where forms first tested themselves out, embodying hope as they did so.

The past of the sea, the past at the sea's edge, is the most reliable thing in the world – and also the most violent, infinite, distant, inaccessible.

Can we say 'thing' here? Yes, the sea isn't an object. I think we ought to say 'thing'. The sea is the lost thing that's constantly returning. The sea returns endlessly. It keeps constantly upstream from life. It is pure undertow.

*

The two people I walked with for hours and hours: my grandfather Charles Bruneau in the Ardennes forest where, afflicted with Alzheimer's disease, he would lose himself with me; Emmanuèle Bernheim everywhere, in the Sahara, in Corsica, at Tunis, at Carthage, at Sousse, on the channel coasts in Normandy, on the Atlantic coasts in Brittany, on the Portuguese coasts and, lastly, on the coasts of the impressive 'dead sea' contained in the word 'Morbihan'.[xxvi]

*

For her, it was the metamorphic element.

She came out totally *transformed.*

On the empty foreshore, amid the silt and seaweed – before her death, after her death – the sea, ever more beautiful, constantly more beautiful, constantly returning, constantly slipping away, still whips up the spray that it wrests from the surface of the waves and hurls it at the face of the one waiting on the shore, onto the forsaken creatures being tanned by the sun, onto the fishers by rod and line and the fishers by shrimp net, onto the mussel pickers, onto all the hikers, all the lovers wandering along the coastal paths or the moonlit paths (and onto Debussy above Dinard), lovers suddenly brought up short by the beauty of the sea, which is engulfing them already with its return.

The sea *rolled up* its waves, the sea straddled *itself*, as much to come back to shore as to abruptly beat a hasty retreat, licking the Earth as it goes. Like a wild boar turning around to face its foe: to brave it, fight and kill. Is there a more intense energy? Like a bull stooping down to show its horns, bellowing in the pen where it has been blinded, starved and brutalised. Is there a difference between the ocean and history? In the former case, it is the precipitancy of what falls back that swells the incoming tide and its own weight sending it crashing against the cliffs or, in the case of history, against human beings. Then what remains of the chalk cliffs, what remains of human civilisations is just a sort of sand or ash that furrows and shifts, rises, soars, swirls, falls again and lands back down on itself. It stacks up, crumbles and rolls. It is in the active suddenness of the moment that these masses, which grind down everything they've carried away, collapse, before disappearing, before melting away as if nothing had happened into the empty, and for us initially natural, then physical, depths of time where it is so dark that they are absorbed without a glimpse of them being possible. How to see a work of art in total darkness.[xxvii]

These depths inaccessible from the sea shores, this anteriority irrecoverable in the haunting vision of the ruins of historic cities, may be seen each night in the darkness that reappears behind the stars, in the depths of the dark itself, which profoundly, etymologically, *siderates* the living and perhaps even *puts it to sleep*. This chasm sucks things down as though siphoned down a hole. Then what is unleashed flows back at the same time, spinning round on itself like a top, and at that point simply becomes the eye that is the axis of the tornado. *Ce siphon est un tiphon* – this siphon is a typhoon. If Chaos is the first of the gods, Typhon is the last of them to appear in Greece. The eye and the hole come together. We are surrounded by great animals, ancestral and inexplicable. What call does the tide obey? To what call does the massacre answer? What drive underlies the huge shaggy mane of the Laniakea Supercluster? What hope do epidemics answer to? What thrust underlies the Virgo Cluster? What is the pain behind the fruit that falls in the beauty of summer? What fascination is the apple – or the fruit Eve took from the garden that lies upstream from the centuries, from the years and the hours – obeying? The garden, which is the joy of the hours and the occasion of beauty in the round of days. Into what vestige of forms does the dream lure us – the dream which lives in metamorphosis the way a fish lives in the water it animates? What call is the song answering to that half-opens the beaks of birds? That unfurls the meaningful language issuing from our lips? What call are these hairline strands of light obeying, which suddenly relegate darkness to the depths of the universe and mitigate the dizziness of those of us who roam upon this fiery crust, which a tiny star, at which we cannot stare directly, is still consuming?

Chapter XXXII

Dates of Thalassa

It was in Hungarian army uniform, while stationed at Pápa in 1914, that Sándor Ferenczi began to write his book *Thalassa*.

The book of the play between darkness and sunlight.

The oh so simple *fort-da* game is not just the play of waves. The play of what goes away and comes back is not just the play of the tides. The play between what is lost and what reappears was no longer just the play of Day and Night: the game of the world of light and solitude had become the game of war.

It is the absent/present game of the Great War to which all adult men were passionately committed, and whose mystery a young child – like a tender, primal shaman – unveiled, as his grandfather looked on, fascinated.

In mid-September 1915 Ferenczi is stationed at Györ. At the moment Sándor Ferenczi, sitting in a tent erected on the banks of the Ruba, is finishing his magnum opus on the metamorphoses of matter, of the sea, of life and of eros driving the world, Sigmund Freud leaves Berchtesgaden and travels to Hamburg: to his daughter Sophie's home at 18, Parkallee. Freud observes his eighteen-month-old grandson Ernst playing a game with his absent father who was fighting on the French front. One is reminded of Friedrich Nietzsche, also on the French front and in a Prussian uniform, writing *The Birth of Tragedy* while garrisoned at Metz with the occupying army after Germany's remarkably rapid victory over France in the war of 1870.

On his return from Hamburg, Freud meets up with Ferenczi at Pápa in the Hungarian forest, where Ferenczi submits the first German version of *Thalassa* to an enthusiastic Freud.

There is a fine photo of Ferenczi dressed in his Hungarian army uniform, in the company of a small black dog, at the edge of the forest.

On 23 February, the father of little Ernst, whose name is Max Halberstadt, is seriously wounded. He is hospitalised at Valenciennes.

*

The ocean covers seventy per cent of the surface of the globe we call terrestrial.

*

Thalassa is, in my view, the finest book psychoanalysis has produced. It proved a terrible strain on Ferenczi to draft the essay, though it is not, in the end, very long. He had moreover great difficulty writing it in his native language, his mother tongue Hungarian, then translating it into German, the language of his medical profession, for Freud's reading and approval.

For one has, at a certain moment, to pass from the mother to the father.

Every work, before being published, awaits an authorisation which is in reality, if one thinks about it, entirely mysterious.

Then he felt the need, for a reason which seems even more mysterious to me, to move from German to Hungarian in a second looping-back from the father's language to the mother's, to arrive at the definitive version. This was in Hungary, at Budapest, in 1928. Fourteen years later.

*

The speculative intuition presiding over Ferenczi's essay predates the outbreak of the First World War by a long stretch.

Yet that short book was composed *within* the war. Written twice and re-translated on two occasions. That makes four times. Four versions. In the second year of the First World War.

It is thus that the oceanic found its impossible *place* in the *leisure-hours* of war.

*

Thalassa is the English (and French) title. This perfectly fitting, perfectly sublime title is not Ferenczi's. The word *thalassa* means ocean in ancient Greek. That is primarily the domain of the god Poseidon, the god of the ocean who hates Ulysses and wishes to see him die as he suffers the interminable ordeal of his impossible return. It is, secondly, the element from which the goddess Venus emerges directly, naked and dripping, truer than Truth, from the genitals of her grandfather which have been severed by his son Chronos, using his sickle, and spilled into the ocean.

The German title is *Versuch einer Genitaltheorie* – An Essay on the Theory of Genitality. It was by this title that the book was known when it was first published in Vienna after the First World War.

The Hungarian title is darker: Catastrophes in the Evolution of Sexual Life. This marvellously tragic title is almost narrative. It is the title of the definitive version.

A man formed the desire to make contact with that which lived before life. He wanted to put his finger on what has existed obscurely within us since the dawn of time, on the boundary between cosmic matter and terrestrial life. To address the chance occurrence of the anarhythmetic, excessive time that came into being in birds and animals with dreams, before the psyche can remember its dreams, before thought can think, before language can speak, before death can write.

This man with the sleepy name Sándor – in Hungarian it sounds like the French words *champ d'or* (field of gold) – penetrated that darkness. The name Sándor comes to us from Alexander, who crossed the Hellespont, led his troops across Persia, and advanced into India as far as the banks of the Ganges. He managed to confront the Erstwhile in the depths of time, to go as near as is possible to the 'drive', that sudden urge within the origin of the thrust which drives the past and drives history, prehistory, palaeontology, biology, embryology, chemistry, and physics.

He dived into the wave.

This desire to immerse the human world in the physical source that preceded it was Sándor Ferenczi's from the moment he discovered psychoanalysis. This lasted twenty years. It began as a flash of lightning: an electrocution, a thunderbolt. Then an increasingly wild, increasingly untamed, theory of the genital embrace which by turns inspires him and disgusts him with its crudeness, its unsentimental brutality, its unavowable violence. 'A bad joke', he writes shamefacedly in his letters. He makes his argument to Freud, who immediately lends support to the man who is still his best friend, who supports him unreservedly, and who, with all his might and main, backs up this *vision from the basement*. But Sándor Ferenczi keeps putting off writing the essay. When the first version is finally completed in an army camp at Györ, in the Tatra mountains, the war, which has served as a pretext to write it, serves as a pretext to delay its publication.

In truth, Ferenczi was not only terrified, deep down, by the prospect of losing his credibility as a doctor in the eyes of his colleagues; he also feared he would bring shame on himself among his patients, his nearest and dearest, his fellow citizens, his parents.

In 1919, he attempted a dry run. He condensed the argument of the book into a lecture.

In 1922, he took a further step, in the form of the two papers he delivered at Berlin.

Finally, in 1924, ten years after the declaration of war, he crossed the Rubicon. Though he did so initially in German – in Austria, at Vienna – before daring to confront his own country.

It was not until 1928 that he took the plunge.

*

Freud had drawn on archaeology and ethnology. Ferenczi wished to push the investigation even further back in time.

To throw the anchor-buoy of physical conception as far as possible from shore – into the immensity of the primal ocean.

To plunge the remarkably unstable and fragile psyche that develops in sexed bodies into the genetic mix, the *morphosis* of nature, the *hypnosis* of prenatal life, into the incredible oceanic emotion that precedes all stases, all stages, all states: into the incredible mutation of physical force transforming into 'life' trying itself out on Earth.

A 'natural history of the human condition' surging up from the geology of the Earth, which is itself a sounder science than the diachrony imposed on human time by language in the form of history.

A palaeontology.

Because the greater part of the Earth's past is reengulfed by itself. By way of volcanoes – the mouths of volcanoes – the Earth is constantly swallowing itself back down. The Earth is fed with its own remains. It devours itself in its detritic past, which it reprocesses in its entirety beneath the massed oceans. It gives it constant *rebirth* in ever newer magma. This is how the past becomes Erstwhile: as the earth sinks into itself, it decomposes, melts, boils, becomes mud; the boiling mud becomes lava and the lava surges up again, like the dripping-wet Aphrodite reemerging from the grandfather's severed sex on the surface of the waves.

Like Iceland. Brand spanking new, metamorphic, spattering and spitting its flames, its geysers on the surface of the sea.

Like the mount dedicated to Saint Michael, sitting amid the tides, that sent up its churches, chapels and ramparts into the Breton sky in the eighth century, piling them one on the other, to be topped by the lance and the sword of its intercessor.

Or surging up like Sant'Angelo at the other end of the little island of Ischia, which it bursts through like a child being born – a child that howls out in atmospheric air – and raises its strange dome there in the thirteenth century.

Chapter XXXIII

Resurgences

In the mountains of the Ain region in 2014, the nineteen miles of the Valserine were granted the European designation of 'wild river'.

The god of Europe, Mont Blanc, is visible from there.

These are wonderful riverbanks, steep-sided and noisy, increasingly hirsute. One examines them with reverence. They have become very difficult to get to. But from a distance, a great distance, the song that rings out there can be heard in the untouched, almost primal, almost intact space – were it not for the air, the rains, and we ourselves who claim to protect them by interdicting them, who advance with caution, as silently as possible, with the very movement that excludes us from them.

The water falls.

The 'swallows' or sinkholes the river hollows out and into which it suddenly disappears are called 'pertes' by French geographers. A name that translates as 'losses'.

They put us in mind of death.

Others call them *résurgences* – resurgences.

*

Some memories or wounds take years to come to the surface of our lives. Suddenly, inexplicably, they devastate us like waves hitting out of the blue.

*

In the most arid places, the clouds that are rent apart on the mountain peaks, that pour out their content onto the flanks of those mountains, bubble up again four or five months later at oases in the middle of the desert.

*

I was moving forward in the dark and I said:

'There are things which wound the soul when they reemerge from memory.

Whenever they come back to mind, there is a tightening of the throat.

When you tell of them, it is worse still, since, if you share them with those who look up attentively and listen, little by little they engender:

a pain or, at least, an unease, that intensifies them.
A fear, too, to hear them spoken,
a fear of having heard them told,
a fear to say them.
They bring a quivering to the lips.
The voice falters.
You stop talking.
You stop talking, but then you start writing.'

Chapter XXXIV

Renaissances

The people of the Renaissance knew nothing of the name Renaissance. The learned Italians of the Renaissance asserted very oddly that they had seen returning from the depths of antiquity, and from the depths of the Bosphorus and the port of Byzantium, a goddess of love – and of the sea – springing up from the waves. It seemed to them that Venus was *returning* to the Earth. The Renascent One. The Revenant. And she was returning stark naked. She was incredibly beautiful. In a bold and unfathomable way, at that moment in history, the finest moment of the Middle Ages, thought attempted to disjoin God from Time. A type of ideology, shared by a number of believers, of monks, scholars, translators, musicians, cardinals and princes, took the form of a restoration of the past – even the past before the birth of their God – to change the present.

The Renaissance was the first theorisation of anachrony.

It is not the idea of the future that modifies the present by exerting a retroactive effect on it. It is the past that has to be changed for current reality to be transformed.

Chance or fortune (what *heur* in the word *bonheur* means) is a better source for future 'becoming' than the intents of a God.

But how can the gates of paradise be reopened without something being torn up? How can we unstitch the wound? How can we start again from zero dealing with the trauma when the wound healed up so long ago? How can we tear apart, thread by thread, fragment by fragment, the swollen, fragile lips of the wound?

The Protestant Luther, who was surely the greatest man of the Renaissance, wrote: 'Our age is *the breaking of the final seal of the Apocalypse*.'

*

In 1550, it was Vasari, a painter from the mountain village of Arezzo and a student of Michelangelo's, who first used the expression *Il Rinascimento* to refer to a new way of depicting space with more depth within the visible surface.

*

All somatisation is an active, current transmigration of past time, that is to say of time long since disappeared into the flesh.

Jacques Amyot in France, in the sixteenth century after Christ, translated metempsychosis as *transanimation.*

Saint Francis of Assisi received his Erstwhile in the palms of his hands. He discovered it on the tops of his feet after twelve hundred years. The lance of the centurion Longinus took twelve hundred years to pierce the side of the naked saint amid the snow and brambles on the hillside.

Not only did he remotely receive the Passion of his God, but also his Nativity: it was Saint Francis who invented the crib, with its jointed figures, its straw, its ox and ass, which brought prosperity to the port of Naples in the century after his death.

*

In the same way, the doctrine of metempsychosis conceived on the banks of the Ganges in India took twelve hundred years to reach the islands of the Japanese archipelago, following the coasts of China and the thousand shores of Indonesia. At last, more than a thousand years later, it arrived in the port of Fukuoka.

*

Over the course of time, there are reappearances that are no more contemporary than were their ancestral states.

If time is the reference among referents, it is never the contemporary of anything.

The 'drive' has no orientation.

It is as unoriented as was the original implosion in the depths of the heavens.

As unpredictable.

*

The real is the unpredictable.

And the unpredictable defines time.

*

In September 1878, Émile Littré translates Dante's *Inferno* into fourteenth-century French verse. Early in 1879, Littré, whose real first name was Maximilien, having been born at the height of the Terror, but who was transfigured into Émile in the first years of the Empire, adds a melancholy preface to the translation he has just completed: 'What is the point of translating an old Italian poem into a French that would itself require translation?'

This is each of our lives.

*

In the last years of Roman antiquity, the Emperor Marcus Aurelius wrote in Greek in Book 7 of his *Meditations*: 'You are allowed to relive. You should even live everything as though you were reliving it.' We might translate this, alternatively, as: 'It is possible to live twice'.

In other words: it is possible to write.

For translating and being reborn are the same. Such is the hope of analysis: to translate what was, to revive the living beneath what has gone extinct. The volcano beneath Virgil's garden.

Chapter XXXV

The Livres d'Heures of Love

He always fought without any hope of winning the battle, without fooling himself about the outcome, without the slightest illusion about the war he was waging. He waged it out of fidelity to the ideas of the women he loved. Even in the year 1652, so full of daring exploits, in which he momentarily lost his sight, his bold moves had no prospect of success. They were strange and downright suicidal, mere empty acts of noble sentiment.

Vinyl records which you interrupt at the finest moment, break over your knee and throw into the waste basket – such are his maxims.

Prayers which, in moments of desire, one holds back in the depths of one's being, hopes which one dares not air to the gentle, delicate ears of one's loved one – Geneviève de Longueville – but which one's mouth nonetheless pronounces and to which one's body bends.

*

He told his sister he had no calling from God, but that what actually drove him was disgust with the world. On the night of 23–24 November 1654, meditating on a page from John's gospel – which he subsequently had sown into the clothes he was wearing when he died – he decided to leave. He left on 7 January 1654 for Port-Royal des Champs to be with his sister Jacqueline who had left on 4 January two years previously. The cold drives them both. The brother and the sister are inseparable. He moved into the Duc de Luynes's château de Vermurier first, before finding himself a room at the Ferme des Granges, outside the abbey walls, at the top of what the nuns called 'the mountain'.

*

Over his despair, his life and his passions, La Rochefoucauld drew a decent veil, maintained a respectable silence. Benjamin Disraeli, Earl of Beaconsfield, said: 'Never explain, never complain.' La Rochefoucauld said, 'The more excuses one makes, the more one compounds one's offence.' 'May this body die, confined as it is in a cage *like a historian*!' That was the way Alexander preferred to put it, speaking of

Callisthenes. He wrote little but always in a frenzy. He loved the noblest, most complex, most difficult, most valiant of women. He raised the language into which he was born to the finest pitch it had known since its inception - since Nithard the chronicler wrote on the Strasbourg plain, beside the river Ill, on Friday 14 February 842. He tore the veil of Maya from top to bottom, once and for all. The systematic fever that animated La Rochefoucauld and Esprit will transmit itself to Schopenhauer, then to Nietzsche, then to Freud in the second half of the nineteenth century.

*

There are few examples of such a fierce commitment. The system of Epicurus transformed by Lucretius's poem. The Buddhist parables in their Japanese Zen version. The thought of Nietzsche transfigured and ennobled by Bergson's version, then subsequently darkened in the hands of Heidegger. Freud's system transformed by the companionship and genius of Ferenczi and finally reworked in the infernal version produced by Melanie Klein, Jacques Lacan and Maria Torok.

*

One is often obliged to continue in a calm, composed way what one began in anger. This was the case with his love for Geneviève de Bourbon, Duchesse de Longueville, from 1646 onwards (she gave him a son in the night of 28 January 1649). At the height of battle, they sent each other their *livres d'heures*, bound in green if the answer was yes. Then the one or the other of them would re-stable their horse. They got mixed up about the colours the way Aegeus did when he was misled by seeing a white sail and believed his son to be dead. Aegeus who threw himself into the sea that took his name.

In 1651, he is at Le Havre, looking out to sea.

Froberger is composing his *Méditation sur ma mort future*.[xxviii]

In July 1652, wounded in one eye on a barricade in the Faubourg Saint-Antoine, La Rochefoucauld loses his sight. Blancheroche dies the following month. He meets Madame de La Fayette. The sight returns in one eye. Love for Madame de La Fayette (twenty-one years younger than him) only begins, only emerges, only takes off truly in 1655. She hated leaving her apartment, crossing the threshold, taking a step into the daylight, into the world: even to get to the gondola bearing the duke's arms that was moored at the quai des Augustins; even to give herself to her lover and sink her face into his hands. She preferred the pain of her regret, not eating, never eating, weeping for the absent one who was absent only because she feared his presence. It was far less a question of weeping for him than of dreaming of him in the void. Neither separated nor united, the two of them, Madeleine and François, meet in the private mansion on rue de Seine.

There is suffering from which one dies, he notes, and for which solitude readies us.

In 1670, the duke could no longer walk. In 1672, Madame de La Fayette, herself ill, retired to Fleury-Meudon. The duke remains alone in his mansion on rue de Seine. 'He is unbelievably sad', writes Madame de Sévigné to her daughter.

*

On the first of January 1675, Madame de Thianges gave her nephew not a *livre d'heures* but a strange sort of 'crib' as a New Year's present. It consisted of wax figures conversing in a tiny salon: together, they represented *la Cabale du Sublime*. La Rochefoucauld is there, alongside Bossuet. Madame de La Fayette sits in a fine upholstered armchair while a short distance away, Jean Racine and Jean de La Fontaine are hand in hand. They are whispering to each other, as though at Tenebrae.

Then his mother dies, and his son the Prince de Marcillac is seriously wounded at the crossing of the Rhine. Then his son the Chevalier de Marcillac is killed, at the same time as the other son he had with Madame de Longueville. On 15 April 1679, she dies. On 16 March 1680, he dies.

*

Love is the only unmotivated motivation that relates directly to the *élan* of life.

It is *l'heur* – fortune.

'Who is as *mal-heureux* – un-fortunate, unhappy – as he thinks? Who is as *heureux* – happy – as he had hoped?'[xxix]

The announcement of a mortal illness that afflicts us suddenly *marks out* the shadow of paradise.

*

This strange shadow cast around us sets a seal upon what will be lost, but in so doing, it renders it glorious. The way it is splendidly and unexpectedly thrown into relief matters more than the mere count of days still left to live. It is curious that we can describe this count as a kind of Eden. The line cast by the shadow etches the borders of a world lost in the real. By leaving this shadow on the diminishing expanse of days, death brings with it a place, or it at least creates a shore; a space we can no longer pass beyond. A kind of pale, weak light rises over this sublime expanse, into which the finest or most cherished part of what we have lived is now concentrated. In this threat suddenly overtaking everything, some stretches of landscape make their own appeal to the heavens. It is possible that the body is staking a claim to that world long lost, which superimposes itself on the one we shall abruptly have to leave. That world long gone, of water and shadow, of sounds subdued and slow, of the first glimmers of light, is much vaster than the mother who did nonetheless containe it, and who is herself long gone. That space which is not yet hollowed out by the shadow of things that have not yet happened, which has not yet elevated what it has nevertheless attained: here is yet a sort of harbour, a sort of bay, a sort of haven I wished to see figure in the last of my days by recording them, hour by hour, as so many joys.

Chapter XXXVI

The Girl in the Ashes

Cinderella slept for a hundred years.

On the bed she moves her arm, she opens her hand, her mind awakens.

The spindle on the bedspread falls. And as she raises her arm and sits up, the dress that covered her also turns to dust. She is filled with shame at being seen denuded as she sits on her bed. Her robe of dust spills on to the floor.

She covers her beautiful breasts with her arm.

Once out of bed, she cups her other hand over her sex.

Then she is seized by fear.

Whose faces are these?

Her friends, male and female, and her parents aren't there anymore. Why aren't they?

Where is her beloved? The prince, who would be 120 years old now, died long ago in the dense forest. All the horses, so marvellously accoutred, are skeletons lying among the leaves. All hawks have vanished from the sky. The gauntlet on which they used to land lies in tatters on the stool. The dogs she loved neither nestle, sighing, at her feet nor bump their heads against her legs in shows of affection.

She picks up the crystal glass at her bedside: the wine is sour.

The logs in the fireplace are now just a loose, dark sand.

Manners, tastes, food and knowledge have changed. She is at a loss. It is so painful to suffer the presence of an ancestral – terribly ancestral – mind in a twenty-year-old body that she bursts into tears.

*

A little of this *time malaise* can still be felt when you get on a plane.

Something within time overtakes our sense of time's passing.

In its breathing and the regular movements of the heart, the life inside a living body feels unease at time getting ahead of itself. This time sickness experienced by humans on long flights – and likewise on the long voyages that are bouts of depression – is known in English as *jet lag*.

*

Can it be painted, this leaving which returns without really returning?

Can we give visible form to a sense of waiting that is never allayed, which the proximity of death only heightens?

You can paint an hourglass, a candle, a skull, a fruit, a butterfly, a 'language of the hours' – a *horologion* – a sundial and the shadow of its steel gnomon, a watch with a shiny chain, a dripping clepsydra.

You can paint a man picking up a scythe and cutting the hay – a *fenisex*.

You can paint Saturn devouring a child, holding him by the leg and chomping into the flesh of his neck as he screams and gesticulates.

But that does not paint time: it paints symbols of time, symbols which remain outside time's flow.

What content contains its container?

The time that contains space has no container.

*

The solid seed – the inner core – at the metallic heart of the Earth dates from 1936.[xxx]

*

In this sense, we cannot even say of this world – of all the creatures living on the Earth, of all the beings on it that we desire, of all those that die, of all the landscapes spread out on it – that the regime is one of non-presence. We should say more exactly, the regime is one of *non-contemporaneity*. Similarly, the reference point for the verbal modalities of human languages precedes them by several tens of millennia in cries and breaths and winds. Inconcomitance reigns everywhere, including within a single system, including within the wondrous pocket of the heliosphere. And this is also why every civilisation distinguishes itself from a society by ritualising an earlier, different, sacrificed, dead language which it then venerates in the form of the writing used to re-transcribe the current spoken language. In the French word *jadis*, meaning in former times, once upon a time, the *Ja* always has *dies* (day) in its nocturnal *chaos*. 'Once' *upon a time* always reigns over every myth and shapes it. But precisely 'once'. That *one time* has never had the good fortune (*l'heur*) to remain there as a present with time's consent. The *jadis*, the Erstwhile, always takes the form of emergence in the form of a *revenant*, including within the mother's uterine cavity. These strangely equinoctial nights. Dreams always make the dreaming body erect. Hence the ultimate aporia specific to the Erstwhile. How can the Father find a footing in the Real? He cannot. There is never a father. Only sons faced with a missing ancestor, and that absence seeks representation in the eyes of the smallest who are born, without his ever making an appearance.

We may even say that it is this feature, this 'He cannot' – that defines death.

*

The moon takes its colour, pale and sublime, from a sun the Earth cannot see.

Chapter XXXVII

Poems

Bulls live thirty years and frogs too;
the tortoise a hundred and fifty;
a wasp five.
Sturgeon live a hundred years; the sponge, fifteen; the mouse, three;
man comes between the goose - or the swan - and the farmed mussel.
Lions, the kings of nature, live no more than thirty-three years; pigeons thirty-five; vultures a hundred and twenty. We are going up. We are rising in time and in age.

*

1879, the eight-year-old Maria, lifting her head, banging her head, looking at the ceiling and raising her hand, shouted:

'Mira, papa! Bueyes!' (Look, daddy! Oxen!)

Altamira had appeared, though it took years and years for people to be convinced of it.

Cave art is so recent in humans' dark, cavernous, sooty cephalic cavities.

*

King Arthur never saw a hydrangea.

Anne de Bretagne never knew wisteria.

The first horse-chestnut tree arrived in Paris, transported from Asia Minor by a square-rigged caravel in a bamboo chest that had been placed on the poop deck. Four sailors carry it onto a cart drawn by two oxen on the cobbled streets of Le Havre. We are in 1612.

*

In 1954, a Uigur Shaman began to drum with all her might on her goatskin.

An ethnologist, who was standing by the yurt, untied her bag and immediately recorded her.

Back in Moscow, when she ran the tape, the young ethnologist realised that the shaman was speaking to Canxila. She transcribed all that the woman said.

The Uigur shaman of 1954 was conversing with the daughter-in-law of Genghis Khan.

Having begun to spin round extremely fast on one foot, still hammering on her drumskin, she had muttered the ritual incantation: 'All that gushes from the mountain caves, all that rushes down in a mighty stream, all that pre-ordains rebirths and returns. Pool of water before the sea, shoot before the tree, fawn before the deer, waterfall on rocks, cave in the mountain – everything about us wells up again from the depths of the Earth. The crystal gods are in darkness.'

But after she had mumbled these words required for the releasing of visions, suddenly she threw back her head. A wonderful song about the Erstwhile rose from her lips.

Impossible to tell who is singing: the shaman or the queen.

Seven hundred and fifty years after her own death, she hums the words: 'I am very old. I know nothing any more. I reel from one ancestor to another, spin from coupling to coupling, fissure to fissure, crevice to crevice, cave to cave. The pure water I hold between my lips refreshes faces.'

*

In 1663, the manuscript of the *Cena Trimalchionis* was rediscovered by chance. At that point Monsieur de

Saint-Évremond chose Petronius as his hero. He translated him. He published him. Then he fled Île de la Cité – to avoid dying as Petronius had done, on Nero's orders, in the Bay of Naples. He abandons his horse at Dieppe, boards a sea-going barge, crosses the Channel, sails along the English coast, lands at Hastings, travels up the Thames in a large river barge and reaches London, where his lingering death takes forty years.

*

Eleven vessels approached the coasts of Massachusetts. One of the captains was called Dickinson. He settled at Amherst.

Chapter XXXVIII

The Palace of Versailles in the Snow in 1991

The official car stopped, skidding slightly on the cobblestones beside the steps up to the north wing of the Palace. It was winter. I walked cautiously into the flurry of snow. As always – and like all obsessives – I was early. The man I was there to see – like all powerful people – was late. It was very cold. There was a layer of frozen snow on the cobbles. The driver helped me climb the stairs up to the porter's lodge. Thanks to François Mitterand, I had founded a festival of baroque opera, religious music, dance and theatre at the Palace of Versailles. I could wander at will through the endless corridors. I roamed through the empty halls, accompanied only by the key-holder. Alone in the immense Hall of Mirrors, wholly empty and silent, I stared out, as night fell, on the frozen ornamental pools, the leafless trees where snow had curiously piled up, their frailest branches threatening to break. How beautiful it was, Versailles in the snow! Each time I met with a delay – with someone exerting their power – I took the opportunity to dream. It suddenly occurred to me that wild boar might come running out of the forest around the palace gardens, given how intensely cold it was and how hungry they must be. Or deer. Deer anxious at the noiselessness that snow brings, when cold has fully petrified the site. Where were we? When were we? I felt as though I were in a Japanese tale, so tiny in the outsized gallery, inside the great cloud of swirling snow. Was I in Kyoto? Was I in Katsura? Night fell abruptly on all this whiteness. I sat down on an attendant's stool staring out at the darkness that had now enveloped the enormous grounds. Years earlier, Philippe Beaussant, Françoise Sempermans and I had revived the chapel chantry. A stone's throw from the chapel was Gabriel's Opera House.[xxxi] It was the last *Opéra à machines* surviving in France from the Baroque world. Everything had remained as it was since Queen Marie-Antoinette married King Louis XVI. The hand of the Chevalier Gluck, who had written Eurydice's song, was still touching mine. Sade was as yet unacquainted with prison walls.

*

I went down into the stage machinery one day and I

was thunderstruck. To do so was to descend into a world that had known neither the Great Terror nor the other Terrors that had ensued. It was also to descend into a large Piranesi drawing. The auditorium, which, though not visible from there, could be imagined in the space, had been designed like the hull of a great upturned Renaissance caravel. It was a giant's open palm in which the visible, manifest opera house, properly so-called, was merely a walnut. That little *nut* in its brown husk had survived undamaged through two revolutions, two empires and three Franco-German wars. You can't always run away from a treasure. For so many years I had harboured *a dream of a voice from beyond*, the voice of a Sybil at the gates of Hell, of a Siren on a rock, of a child's voice too that would rise up, that would sound out in the space beyond wars and cries and transformations and deaths. A dream of a voice metamorphosed, sung, exhibited, written, driven to extremes, castrated, denuded – a fluid thing that moves one to tears. It was a dream into which all the arts flowed without ever aspiring to totality. I did not see myself as Wagner at Bayreuth. But I would happily have been Handel in London. I would have left behind the press and publishing. I would have gone on writing books, booklets, tragedies, films, Noh plays, Butoh pieces, ballets, requiems and operas. I speak now of what was the bitterest failure of my life. I was imagining this gigantic transformation machine designed by Gabriel becoming once again the essential destination for all the lyrical tragedies and all the *comédies-ballets* of the European seventeenth and eighteenth centuries that required stage machinery. I would have been the Bergman of this new Drottningholm, ten thousand times finer and a hundred thousand times more legitimate than the small palace built on Lake Mälaren could claim to be in respect of the different continents that had been contemporaries in the rise of the Baroque. At a time when Europe was striving to identify with itself, unifying to the point of creating a common magical currency, this town was to become again a global meeting place for baroque intensity, as it once had been in the eyes of all nations: German princes, Venetians, the Turkish Sultan.

The Royal Opera of the Versailles Palace fell under the aegis of the president of the Republic. François Mitterand had very much liked a novel I wrote about Wurtemberg, because it reminded him of the various escapes he had made from POW camps in Southern Germany early in the Second World War. He was in no way put off by my urge to desert the front of present time or by my reservations about groups of any kind. His own destiny was marked by escape. The Director of the Palace – at the time, Jean-Pierre Babelon – also committed immediately and unreservedly to the project and all the stars seemed to be aligned. And so, what was a museum was to bring back to life the legends surrounding the spectacular 'machination' of the old monarchy.

Legends that had suddenly crumbled to dust after the wonderful writings of Jean-Jacques Rousseau, who had claimed to hate them.

The rocks and trees were to move again.

As soon as Orpheus gave his signal, they were to get up on tiptoe and dance in rhythm.

Chariots would fly.

Medea would spring up into the sun.

Seas would batter the shore at the front of the stage with their angry waves once more.

Palaces would collapse rhythmically, in time to the conductor's baton.

At the end of the twentieth century, theatrical spectacle would at last cease to be naturalistic and become imaginative again.

I had a microphone in my hand. I was standing beside François Mitterand, who was so pale, virtually imperturbable. One bald head beside another. I was always shaky when I had to get up and speak in front of people.

Every age, when it is a living one, revisits the totality of its past and develops a new image of it. In the same way as the Japanese revived noh and kabuki, and brought back Zeami, Zenchiku and Chikamatsu, so Torelli, Vigarani and Berain would be making a return. And so, for this music and these *spectacles à machines* that the Centre de musique baroque was exhuming – the scores of which were being recorded as soon as they had been deciphered and published, the records attracting ever more enthusiasts, the films proving capable of stirring souls anew – millions of people were to beat a path to Versailles once more, after three hundred years; were to return to encounter all these songs, these sermons, these funeral orations, these Tenebrae readings, these mime shows which awaited them like ghosts: in other words, like ancestors. Thus, all lovers of opera and laments, of stunning and solemn choreography and of baroque tragedy would, little by little, come inwardly to desire to visit at least once in their life this place where, hidden away for centuries, above a tiny stage, was the largest, most extraordinary dream machine to have come down to us from that world.

The press pressed and oppressed.

The whale, covered in silver scales, with its brilliant, gold-spangled eyes swallowed Andromeda whole.

One after the other, the trap doors opened together

in synchronised fashion, without even the slightest creaking. The city, the département, the region, the Ministry of Culture, the Prime Minister's office and the Centre de musique baroque all betrayed the venture. Only Mitterand, Babelon and I still held on to the desire. The Ministry of Finance forced an inquiry on us. They questioned me. I abruptly brought together the board of trustees. I was exultant but did not show it. I announced simply: 'I'm dissolving the festival and I'm going too.' I took the opportunity to resign from the Centre de musique baroque. To relinquish the presidency of Jordi Savall's Concert des Nations. To initiate a general withdrawal from official or social functions of any kind, including those I had performed in publishing since 1969. The subsidy was officially signed off on 20 January, and by 16 February all debts were cleared. At that point I was overwhelmed by the urge or the haste to bid farewell to everything.

*

Yet, the idea behind the festival was not at all mad. I still believe in the project I had nurtured, and consider it possible, even today, despite having failed to see it through. In a first phase, by creating a Centre for Baroque Music, the jewel of Baroque architecture was adding in all the luxurious, musical, entertaining, spectacular and emotional delights of the Court to which it was dedicated. In a second phase, we were adding the *opéra à machines*, the *ballet à machines* and the *théâtre à machines*, thanks to the auditorium designed by Ange Gabriel, with its mechanical workings and metamorphic capacities restored. In a third phase, I would have liked to bring back into the chapels and churches of Versailles, to Notre-Dame de Versailles and to Saint-Louis Cathedral, not only the art of sacred oratory but, most importantly, the Tenebrae services which, as I saw it, formed the essence of the French Baroque.

Couperin on an equal footing with Bossuet.

Each letter is snuffed out, its shape consumed individually, as incredible musical arabesques and responses are echoed back from the darkened nave. The bells fall silent. The statues are covered with a purple veil. Jeremiah laments the siege and sack of Jerusalem by Nebuchadnezzar's army in 586 BC.

Jean de la Fontaine, barely a religious man, always accompanied Racine to the service of Tenebrae on a Friday. He knelt by his side. He wept. He wept over the death of the dead god. It was, for him, beauty in its pure state. Tenebrae was the French *noh*.

Chapter XXXIX

The 1640s

In 1979 I wrote: 'I hope to be read in 1640.' This made the headlines of a magazine. In pronouncing these words, I was defending as best I could the eight volumes of *Petits Traités* I was writing at the time.

These fictional snippets, these etymological puzzles, these fragments of autobiography, these small bits of essays had all come to hover around that date, 1640, that is somehow foundational in my life, though of what I do not know. Of nothing. Initially, as I saw it, it was a memory from my primary schooling in the then totally ruined François-I Lycée for Boys at Le Havre. We were taught in huts. I was a choirboy in the chapel destroyed by the US Air Force. 1640 was a date printed in bold type in a summary at the bottom of the right-hand page of our green history book, a thing we had to learn by heart for the next lesson. The sentence ran as follows: 'It was in 1640 that the first *louis d'or* were struck in France.' That date came to be the focus of – came to absorb – all my daydreams, like a black hole in an imaginary sky.

*

It isn't just in Japan that people bring out benches to stare into the night.

*

Above and beyond the golden *louis* coin, 1640 saw the publication, in the city of Louvain, of *Augustinus* by the bishop of Ypres, who signed his name Jansenius.

Cornelius Jansen was a fellow student and later bosom friend of the Abbot of Saint-Cyran.

Jansen dies during the plague epidemic in May 1638, two years before his book is published.

It was only after the humiliating, painful death of Saint-Cyran himself that the dead Jansen's *Augustine*, published during the Abbot's imprisonment, made its impact.

It was in 1640 that the second year of Saint-Cyran's imprisonment began.

Of Monsieur de Saint-Cyran, his Eminence Cardinal Richelieu wrote: 'I do not know what to say of this man with those sparkling eyes and almost inaudible voice, except that *there are tidal surges that break down dikes*, and it is better to put them away behind prison walls without enquiring into their motives.'

This saying of Richelieu's is worthy of the Duc de La Rochefoucauld.

*

In 1640 France was occupying Savoy. That is why I wrote *L'Amour conjugal.*[xxxii]

In 1640 France participated in the Portuguese uprising. I wrote *La Frontière*,[xxxiii] which I published first at Lisbon, in Pedro Tamen's translation, with a scholarly note by José Meco.

Then the entire city of Paris erupts in revolt with barricades everywhere. The Fronde sets France ablaze. I wrote *L'amour la mer.*[xxxiv] April 1652 sees the Great Terror with Parisians fleeing the city. This is the so-called Day of Straws.[xxxv] La Rochefoucauld is wounded in the eye in the assault on the Porte Saint-Antoine. He locks himself away in his darkened room and gathers his thoughts, the reverberations of a time of turmoil. August 1652 sees the death of Monsieur Blancheroche, who falls backwards down his staircase in rue des Bons-Enfants with Johann Jakob Froberger looking on, the latter immediately composing a short *tombeau* on an absurd death. That *tombeau* is the first *suite française*. It seemed to me that the time that was theirs and the time that was coming upon us were the same time.

*

The Strasbourg *Great Vanity* was painted by Stoskopff in 1640.

*

King Louis XIII, who liked to rest at dusk on a chaise longue which he called his 'Roman couch', took down in 1640 all the paintings in his bedroom, except for Georges de La Tour's *Saint Sebastian*, which stayed on the facing wall in his Louvre palace. It was a painting that he loved greatly, as much for the beauty of the naked body depicted as for the dense, calmly borne grief to be seen on the doomed man's face.

*

To hope that what one wrote in 1979 would be read in 1640 was to reverse not the direction of time, since it has no direction, but the customary sense of that orientation.

It was to wrest all continuity from the supposed or atrocious or derisory or superstitious progress of history.

It was – and still is – to open up one's life to the unforgettable ruin of time.

To cite is to ruin.

Everything that becomes its own referent is a ruin, when that referent has come adrift, been unseated, unharnessed.

Everything that has an eye to its own emancipation, everything seeking to break the ties, throw off the shackles, shatter the yoke – everything readying itself for freedom – is a ruin.

*

'1640' is the name I give to the mental vacuum that followed the collapse of Renaissance Europe, plunging it back suddenly and entirely into civil and religious war.

*

On 7 September 1640, Descartes's daughter dies at Amersfoort, aged five.

Chapter XL

The Hours Torn from the Book

The *Essays* Montaigne wrote might be called *Atmosphere of Saint-Bartholomew's Day.*

He played a part in the deliberate forgetting of a monstrous event. This is what, nowadays, we call 'denial'. A group of men wished to be loyal to the king. Those men, who, among themselves, went by the name 'humanists', decided to expunge the date of the Saint Bartholomew's Day Massacre. Not only did they resolve to do this, but they swore an oath to eradicate that date from the course of time.

*

The night of 24 August 1572.

On the stroke of midnight, the bells of Saint-Germain-l'Auxerrois, a church to the eastern side of the Louvre, give the signal for the massacre.

King Charles IX himself opens his window and fires

off his harquebus into the night.

*

Why was the page for 24 August torn out of Montaigne's journal, which is a universal chronology known as the 'Beuther', a present from his father, and is preserved in the limpid, luminous, glacial, conditioned air of the Bordeaux municipal library's Reserve Collection? Who tore it out? It was not time that did so. Why did Montaigne reach out his hand? Why did he tear it out one day? Why did he rip *that particular day* out of his great book of hours? Why did he tear out the only day that ought to have been remembered?

*

Time has to be *opposed* radically to space, as Bergson did in his day: Bergson conceived that opposition at just the moment when Freud was starting to write.

Space is the *second time.*

Space is what time extends into after its implosion. It is the coldness into which it subsides. It is collapsed time in the darkness traversed by a faint light whose source is long dead even though we tremble before it, or strain our eyes toward it, as flowers do.

The earliest time is a watery one – then we are expelled into space, where we fall with it.

*

In 1892, Marcel Proust was *garçon d'honneur* (best man) when Henri Bergson married Louise Neuburger.

In 1905, Henri Bergson went to the Père-Lachaise cemetery for the burial of Madame Jeanne Proust, aged fifty-six. He took a weeping Marcel gently in his arms and kissed him in silence.

*

Space is the time that has passed into time and pours out into it.

Space is the time that has found an abode before it dissolves, crumbles, fragments.

Achenes, seeds that fly.

The celandine's powder trail on which the swallow draws as an aid to sight.[xxxvi]

Spores in the dark sky.

Bergson was not kissing time lost (*le temps perdu*), which he could not imagine, but the sweet substance of the past: his *garçon d'honneur*, who had grown up and sprouted a beard like a rabbi's on his cheeks.

Chapter XLI

Jean Bruneau

My uncle so thin, so thin when he came back from the Dachau camp. The time it took him to come back into time!

The light years he had to travel to be back with us.

*

My remarkably thin uncle, who rescued me from my childhood.

*

My uncle so thin, so handsome, handsome as an Annunciation angel, who relaxed in the squat armchair by the corner of my grandmother's pale brown Erard upright piano.

Who sucked with such pleasure on the tip of his rediscovered cigarettes.

His eyes so blue, his metal-rimmed glasses so round.

His head wreathed in the halo of smoke, in its curling and winding, in strange tendrils of light, the smoke fraying on the pale mahogany wood and the big, yellowing, four-handed scores lying open.

*

My young uncle who guzzled all day. Who was constantly bringing out of his waistcoat pockets black liquorice whips with a pearl in the middle.

Pink bubble gums wrapped in the photos of footballers.

Gumdrops.

Brown liquorice roots full of yellow dust, *Gauloises bleues*, little cardboard Italian matchbooks where I was allowed to tear off the strip and light the match, rubbing very hard with the fleshy part of my finger.

*

When the deportees came back from the camps, did they come back? Where did they come from? Where were they going? In what age were they living? Were they still really living? We looked at them and, when we did so, they were painful to see. What we had in front of us was indelible time that certainly had something of death about it, but they were alive. At least, still a little bit alive. We could not but be critical of them for having suffered what they had suffered without dying. They reproached themselves with the same thing vis-à-vis all the people they had left behind in the other world. They suffered the reproach of having remained alive like inassimilable memories of what we would have preferred to omit from history.

The *hibakusha.*

The outcasts.

Their presence – this incarnation that can be seen in Rustin's painting, in which I suddenly saw again my uncle Jean trying to be reborn, struggling with such difficulty and for so long to be reborn when he came back from the Dachau camp, silent beneath the standard lamp, under its two-tone fringes – or, rather, tassels – beside the piano.

*

The *hibakusha*, for whom I played in 2018 on a magnificent Bechstein grand dating from before the bomb, in the little concert hall at Nagasaki.

*

My uncle so thin, so raw-boned, so emaciated, so elegant, who managed to teach me to eat and speak again in rue Marié-Davy where my grandmother had taken me in, exfiltrating me from my own family – how he disrupted the present!

How that disruption of the present, my grandmother, my terrified, starved uncle and their four-handed duets on the piano, protected me!

*

Their difficult survival, which had something impossible about it, made one both incapable of – and as if stunned to be – living. Terror-stricken at having to live again.

*

They were not like Ulysses. Not like sailors returning to their home port.

They were not like memories reforged at their source.

That regain a lost place.

The returners of an unachievable return.

It was not a *nostos*. It was a riving.

Inside the wound of this riving was a new era.

A new primal era and a decisive new light cast on the illusion of the species (legend and utopia), on the dizzying ruination of humanism (faith and progress), on the secular transmission of past values (dead languages, traditional songs, religious rites, decimated and lost peoples), on the tradition of human experience and education in the customary ways of dwelling (nuclear bombs, devastated nature).

*

Some people experience a violent pleasure in disillusion, a pleasure tinged with powerful bitterness.

The everyday expression of 'scales falling from one's eyes' is an oddity.

That expression suggests that we used to be fish: and it is true that we used to be fish.

Saint Paul fell on the road to Damascus. The painter named Caravaggio depicts him thrown backwards under his horse's belly, in the dust of the road, dazzled by a sudden light of unknown source. Dazzled to the point of being robbed of his sight. His horse, after unseating him, runs off. Pulling him by the hand in the dust, his companions drag the young Tarsus rabbi behind them along the sandy track leading to the city of Damascus. Saul stays there three days, blinded and neither eating nor drinking, in a room plunged into darkness. Ananias is called for. There, in Judas's house in Straight Street,[xxxvii] Ananias lays his hands upon him. The Acts of the Apostles adds: '*Confestim ceciderunt ab oculis eius tanquam squamae*. And immediately there fell from his eyes as it had been scales.'[xxxviii]

Some human beings wish to experience this sensation of the scales 'falling' from their eyes, when the real itself suddenly 'falls' under their gaze.

Chapter XLII

Lucretius

The sensation of being disabused is so intense that some may eagerly seek it out.

Hidden beneath the disappointment, there is an 'I knew it!' like a drawn blade suddenly flashing. All of a sudden it is brand new as the knifepoint touches the skin. It is against our will that this fleeting, blinding light bursts into the dense and dulled opacity of our lives. Instantly it illuminates the enigma of our genital origin. This illumination is born of the obvious fact of unforeseeable abandonment by the mother, who abruptly propelled us into the suffocation of birth, throwing us out so violently to be irradiated by the senseless light of the solar system. It accompanies our apprehension of death as soon as we leave the water, as soon as we cry out, as soon as we feel hunger, regret, aloneness and desire.

We then experience an extraordinary, unquenchable curiosity for the pain that birth induced in us from this light: and it is true that that pain *opened our eyes* at the very moment it racked our lungs.

Just as that grief and pain impress their stamp on us in the same instant we approach light's shore – emerging from the fissure, seared by the air, blinded by the discovery of a world of brightness, disgorging the cry which, in terror, triggers the working of the lungs – so, too, language, within us, within our now dazzled vision, awaits that light.

Language is wholly in the mourning for lost unity that it *brings to light.*

The pain of eyelids opening violently wide for the first time at each flash of light.

The breach of our defences of love at first sight.

The pain of interminable separation, of the loss of the vulva and water and shade, the humiliation of the most extreme dependency.

The suffering at the incomprehensibility of everything.

The pain of infancy, cruel and safe, cheerful and suddenly dumbfounded, timid, terrified, agitated once more, inquisitive, propulsive, fired with the animality of *infantia* that knows no old age in its impatience, no meaning in its stubbornness.

The pain of faithful infirmity, more faithful than identity itself, more faithful than the sex organ, so different and unstable, that is exposed in boys as soon as they walk upright, at the age when the tottering body achieves that upright stance in silk skirts, in dark flannels.[xxxix]

This pain of pain – this mourning, the word *deuil* being at the root of *douleur* – can no longer call up the breast which, long ago, its cry could at times summon to the lips uttering it.

Mourning awaits, desperately awaits, what is lost.

By its origin, this pain inclines us to clamp our teeth on silence – on the vertiginous greed for silence – more than on truth.

*

Silence like the whale by which Jonah is swallowed after he refuses to journey to Niniveh.

*

Depressive clarity, the clarity of the scales falling like little shells the instant the eyelids begin spontaneously to edge open. Uncontrollable panic, absolute unintelligibility, a sense of shame overtaking suffering, the contingency of everything, the endless bloody scramble of the living devourers of lives and even of any stirring of life, the drawing-back of lips over teeth, of lips over blood-soaked fangs, the terrible derisive laughter by which the group always punishes; in the depths of each and every shy, timid soul, illumination, panoramic vision, lucidity and discernment are linked.

*

Epicurus and Lucretius knew that mixed and powerful sensation of the senses illuminating and overlapping all of a sudden, all at once. They celebrated that combination of anxious deficiency, psychical birth and startled joy.

La Boétie and Montaigne knew it.

Schopenhauer and Nietzsche knew it.

Esprit and La Rochefoucauld knew it.

*

Jacques Esprit was born at Béziers on 22 October 1611. His father was a physician who practised in the fertile, rose-red city of Toulouse. His elder brother, abbé Thomas Esprit, was an Oratorian priest, who has the adolescent come up from Toulouse to Paris in the summer of 1629 to enter the seminary, where he is received as a novice on 16 September 1629.

Five years later, however, in 1634, the young man leaves the seminary, rejecting the idea of holy orders. Something else preys heavily on his mind.

Esprit had such an attractive face that Germain Habert, the abbot of Cérisy, had been drawn to the handsome child's physique. His conversation was serious and scholarly from the first. He passionately loved to study. Germain Habert provided him with patronage. Chancellor Séguier welcomed him into his house, appointed him tutor to his daughter, obtained for him an annual royal grant of 2,000 livres, had him appointed a Councillor of State and, in 1639, elected to the Académie française.

In 1644, it fell to the Marquise de Sablé to take Esprit under her wing. With the aid of Mlle de Verpillière, she introduced him into the household of the Duchesse de Longueville. Esprit became closely associated with the duchess during the Fronde and struck up a friendship with her lover, the Duc de La Rochefoucauld. In 1649 Esprit accompanies Madame de Longueville to Munster when the Treaty of Westphalia is being negotiated. The following year, after the release of the princes, he is back in Paris and events proceed apace. He becomes a Jansenist like his protectress, and the duchess finds him a post with her brother, the Prince de Conti. Conti takes him to the Languedoc and, unexpectedly, he contracts a marriage with Geneviève Bollain, a beautiful woman much younger than himself, with whom he has already produced three children. On the occasion of their marriage, the Prince de Conti makes him a gift of 40,000 livres and Madame de Longueville adds 5,000 more. They live in rue des Bons-Enfants in Paris, near the house of Monsieur Blancheroche who plays the lute and sells viols. The back entrance to each house looks out onto the Jardin Royal.[xl]

In 1661, as tutor to the Prince de Conti's children, Esprit, returning from Pézenas, meets up again with La Rochefoucauld, who at last is permitted to return to Madame de Sablé's salon after his period of exile. Whenever either travels, they at once write to each other. In 1662, La Rochefoucauld publishes *Mémoires contenant les brigues pour le gouvernement à la mort de Louis XIII*. He begs Jacques Esprit to restore him to the good graces of Madame de Longueville, who is outraged by what her former lover has been so bold as to write. In 1663 a pirate edition of La Rochefoucauld's *Maxims* appears in Holland. He feels deceived and Esprit feels betrayed. Each of the two sees the hand of the other in an affair in which everything is obscure and, certainly, nothing is straightforward. A wounded Esprit packs his bags. Filled with sadness, even disgust, he leaves the capital forever, takes no further part in the Académie's sessions, and goes back to live in the South with his children and Geneviève Esprit, determined to complete the interminable book, his life's work, on the 'falsity' of all the imaginable virtues that men have ascribed to themselves in a world not so very far removed from hell. In 1673 Jacques Esprit writes to Madame de Sablé: 'Madame, I would think I was failing in my duty to you were I not to inform you that I have sent your book to Paris. I call it your book because you are partly the cause of it having seen the light of day, by virtue of the approval you bestowed on it when it was as yet formless.' Five years later, in 1678, aged sixty-six years, on 6 July, Jacques Esprit dies. He died at Béziers just after his book was issued by the bookseller in Paris. The title pages of its two volumes are dated 1678, the frontispiece engraving 1677, the royal approval 24 May 1674, the licence 1 June, the registration of publication 11 June, and the printer's imprint 12 October. Victor Cousin argued that La Rochefoucauld had been Esprit's disciple in terms of thought and his imitator as regards the bleakness of his manner. Sainte-Beuve believed that, though the academician had greatly influenced the duke, the warrior was the source of his own style, since the style of his book in no way differed from the style and intrepidity of his life.

Chapter XLIII

Literature as Cryptography

It so happens that, in the history of France, Jansenist books were the first to be banned before that same censorship was extended to erotic works. Out of this rejection by society, a function emerged, which served first to define them, then retrospectively conferred on both the same aura of liberty and persecution. This is how it came to be that there is, in France, an obscene philosophical space, where language is more raw than it is ordinarily; the radical nature of its argumentation removes masks, in the same way as physical excitation removes clothing: in the same way as God does with the mysterious 'scales' that are our 'eyelids', which close so spontaneously over our eyes when we are swept up by love, in thrall to sensation, engulfed by music, stricken with pain or captivated by dreams.

In the seventeenth century, it was not to the same extent that Jansenists and *libertins* (freethinkers) destroyed fine sentiments.

Two men resolved to leave not a single virtue standing; the two were friends; their names were Esprit and La Rochefoucauld. In the following century, they were Laclos and Sade. The birth of the administration of state censorship simply hid behind the excuse of insults and outrages to the temporal body of the Church and to the newly emergent authority of the monarchy. Monsieur de Harlai spoke of there being 'so many platoons against the state'. The freethinker, the *frondeur*, the *précieuse*, and the Jansenist formed a single opposition to powers that were increasingly centralised and subject to the will of one man who on a winter's day, 23 February 1653, after a night of torchlit revels and dancing, in the still modest palace of Versailles, imagined he had become the sun. A salon in Paris in rue de la Bourbe at the beginning of the 1660s brings them together: the freethinking *frondeur* is François de la Rochefoucauld, the *précieuse* Madeleine de Sablé, and the Jansenist Jacques Esprit. The three functions – the sword; the grieving and distinctly shamanistic woman serving as an intermediary between the living and the world of those 'dead to the world'; the academician employed as a scholarly 'technician', a new Daedalus tasked with giving shape to the 'war machine' – are shared out. The Reformation, the Fronde, preciosity, freethinking, and Jansenism are all alike in not submitting to the usual codes, nor to the genres imposing certain postures, nor to the statutes subjugating destinies. The pure cryptography of literature. It is in the first written work of ancient Greek literature: *On Nature*, which Heraclitus lodged in the temple of the Great Goddess at Ephesus. In the last tragedy that was written: *Cassandra*, which Lycophron slipped into the cubby-holes of the library at Alexandria. In Descartes's writing: *Video ex fenestra pileos et vestes...* I see from this window only hats and coats covering the bones and skulls of the ghosts... *Larvatus prodeo...* I move forward masked because you are merely masks, coats, hats, wigs, face paint, scarves, hollow moans. The *libertin*, the freethinker, refuses to obey the civil proprieties, that which infringes on his independence; the *frondeur* refuses to obey the central power that installs the horror of a tyranny and leads its autonomous administration into the earliest European State; the *précieuse* rebels against the humiliation of a situation in which she is confined to the traditional registers allotted to women, to the servitude of social reproduction, to inadequate education, to rudimentary or simplified use of her language; the Jansenist emancipates himself from the Roman norm of religious experience with the same determination as members of the Reformed Church broke with its mercantile practices; all of them disobey.

The term at the time was 'recalcitrant'.

Also 'Protestant'.

This is why clandestine master-printers who pseudonymously published the sarcastic lampoons by Blaise Pascal or by Pierre Nicole, published obscene prints concomitantly. The finest is by Claude Mellan – though he was not keen to finish it – titled *La Souricière* (the Mousetrap), which imagines the womb of a beautiful woman as the goddess Venus herself, who dooms men to infinite exploration, but also to endless imprisonment and obscurity. And, indeed, the licentious tales reveal the same state of original damnation, the same 'nature', masked by 'art' and beaten down successively by conventions, contracts, families, the various forms of religious practice, absolutism, classicism in all its novelty, and political communities. Neither in Charles de Saint-Évremond nor in René Descartes, neither in Baruch Spinoza nor in Blaise Pascal, can one make out any hint of political secession, scientific struggle, challenge to religion, or mental freedom.

*

Like Hobbes leaving London for Paris and the banks of the Seine, like Saint-Évremond fleeing Paris and embarking for London and the banks of the Thames, like Descartes preferring Stockholm and the islands in the Gulf of Bothnia, like La Rochefoucauld exiled to Vertoeil, his chateau having just been razed to the ground on the orders of the king, they all know, like the feudal aristocratic model defined by Perrault, which he will later dub Bluebeard,[xli] that there is fresh blood on the key, that the key consists solely of this blood that never dries, of this never sublimated savagery; they know that the social secret is war on death making way for rivalry for ranks and for hierarchy in the race for domination: in short, in the reproduction of bodies and in the piercing jealousy of desires. They know, since Hesiod, that Nyx, night, is the daughter of Chaos. That divinity in the god is merely a dream. That all respectability is an illusion, all faith a fable, all power lifting its hand an autocracy beginning to exert its hold. Through withdrawal, retirement, self-abnegation and study, the self acquires freedom from the common language and finds itself in exile, as it were, from the group: as refusal to depend, as sensory singularity, as resistance to all employment, as aversion to all roles, genres, games and masks. 'The late Monsieur Pascal used to say on this subject that Christian piety reduces the individual self to nothing and that human civility conceals and eliminates it.' The *frondeur*, the protestant, the *précieuse*, the freethinker and the Jansenist are secret republicans, feudal duellists who are on the point of being excommunicated, or already imprisoned, or about to be proscribed.

They are, as they said of themselves, if not Asocials, then at least Solitaries.

It is no great distance from a secessive life to a written sentence left hanging.

Such is the first motivation behind fragmentary writing.

The social 'solitary' at Port-Royal is the 'fragment' in classical discourse: they are 'atoms' descending directly from Epicurus via Lucretius. The Romans of the Republic translated the Greek *atomoi* as *individua* in Latin. Such is the individualism of the Fronde. There had been Saint-Évremond atomising Montaigne. There was La Rochefoucauld atomising Saint-Évremond and abruptly pulverising Esprit.

*

They were obsessed with the idea of breaking away. Such are the sublime scenes in which Jacqueline Pascal, in Autumn 1651, is resolved to drop everything and flee. Her father, who has one foot already in the Styx, forbids it. Early in the month of January – on 4 January 1652, at dawn – Jacqueline runs away from her brother Blaise, who is no keener than her father to see her go to the abbey deep in the forest. It isn't often mentioned that the Jansenists of Paris more than once considered imitating the Puritans of London and leaving Europe. In 1620, the first Pilgrim Fathers arriving from Plymouth had disembarked from the *Mayflower* and, in 1630, colonised Massachusetts Bay. In the year of Esprit's death, 1678, the French Jansenists were still in talks to purchase the island of Nordstrand off the coast of Holstein.

Chapter XLIV

Charles de Saint-Évremond

Hobbes's *Surdum est* (It is deaf) was written in 1660.[xlii] Human languages are *deaf* to what they say. There is a secret behind 'signifiance', though its meaning dissipates in a sort of aura or vapour as soon as the mind approaches. A meaning more wary of us than a timid animal. An untamed, and for the most part unconscious, world persists there. It so happens that, even if they are inquiring, simply by speaking, into what they do not know, in the course of dialogue, all human languages range the first and second persons against each other – which thenceforward tear the living world apart, substituting themselves for the lost dyad – and set them up as opposites. They are the I and the Thou, deathless, sexless, genderless and identity-less, which the operation of language imposes on humanity. Thereafter, all words deliver, in their content, something that does not exist, evoking it the way images appear in dreams. In 1661, Monsieur de Saint-Denis de Saint-Évremond goes into exile. He is wanted for duelling, unbelief, disrespect of royal authority, irreverence and licentiousness, and is imprisoned twice on the orders of Cardinal Mazarin. He is hounded out by Colbert, boards a light vessel, crosses the Channel and settles for forty-two years in a small book-lined apartment in London. He becomes a solitary in his own way: he reads. Already surrounded by books, he now surrounds himself with animals, in preference to membership of a *human* court. Reading books in Greek, in Latin, in French; learning to live his life once again in silent writing; silently speaking a language known to none he lives among (in the forty years of his exile, he learned no English); doing his own translation from one dead language to another, one not even spoken where he lives – these were for him one single delight. Sainte-Évremond invents the baroque form of the short treatise, recalling the arborescent chapters of the purely literary essays invented by Montaigne in the late Renaissance, when he was bent upon 'de-dialoguising' Plato, right after his strenuous efforts to 'de-oratorise' his friend La Boétie who had died at Germignan. He shortens them even more. Condenses and prunes them. He dedicates them to Madame de Sablé. He addresses them to Pierre Nicole and sends them to La Rochefoucauld. He corresponds until his dying day with La Fontaine. In his room he feeds over sixty cats, puppies, dogs and birds. He outlives the century. The man baptised at Saint-Denis-le-Gast on the Cotentin peninsula in early January 1614 was buried beneath a slab in Westminster Abbey in late summer 1703. He died refusing the sacraments. There are two sets of his last words. The first is anchoretic and purely defensive: 'that, to die well, he did not need the ceremonies of this world.' The other is an intensely toxic assertion: 'Thinking on Eternity will not occupy the most useless moment of my life.' Des Maizeaux recalled that in the late 1630s, at the Louvre, on the banks of the Seine and beneath the ramparts that ringed Paris, they spoke in fear of Monsieur de Saint-Évremond's boot. He had built himself a system out of system-hatred. 'We do not know ourselves. We are an enigma to ourselves.' It was the early French Baroque that resolved to dispense with grace and conquer melancholy in the almost entropic warmth of demoralisation. A terrible nervous breakdown had almost done for him in 1665, the very year the first edition of his *Reflections* appeared at Paris – or at least the first printing authorised by Monsieur de La Rochefoucauld. To undeceive: the verb summing up his work. Thought is but mendacious stuff, metaphors, ornaments, excess, affectation, indulgence and mirage barely reflecting sensations so much more varied, more profound, more dense, more moving, more alert, more tempestuous. No true meaning resides in the, as it were, immaterial fabric of the spoken language by which women and men, mothers and children, Death and the dying, converse in an endless quarrel. If we leave aside grammar and fear, there is, in truth, no soul within these great clumsy bodies struggling to walk on two feet, which stagger onto boats to cross the waters of the Thames or to disport themselves in wind and rain on the bridges over those waters: this host of women and men moving so oddly, lifting their knees, throwing back their chests advantageously to show their breasts or scrotums, when not at all built to deploy those attributes in space in this way. There is no morality that is not illusory. No sexuality exempted from untameable violence. Desire is endlessly being reborn in the depths of bodies, and it has no fixed object on an Earth that revolves upon itself and circles with the stars in obedience to the more or less continuous, chiral thrust driving them. He published the idea, before Pascal, that there are only distractions. Before La Rochefoucauld, he wrote that narcissism in the world of the spirit, the impulses of the flesh in the world of the body, lust for ownership, and delight in domination in the social world are the motives that inspire the incalculable multitude of actions in reality (that is to say, depredations) and of affections of the mind (that is to say, desires, *envies*). The state of nature is simply the taste for blood, in order to eat, and, at the same time, a fight to the death, in order to survive. The social, fiscal, administrative, juridical state makes it worse, causing the majority to cease fighting for their own interests, in such a way that they atrociously relinquish their strength into the hands of a few. Before Esprit, he wrote that, between human beings, civil society had concluded a pact of confiscated power, which systematically soured into a pact of hatred. This precipitated the chronic succession of vengeful acts that is at the root of history, of which dates make an inventory on a single, interminable, imaginarily-oriented timeline.

*

It so happens that all the creatures who have succeeded in becoming a little freer than others are, sadly, visited by a strange sense of bereavement.

We stole everything.

It is an intermittent sense of guilt, one that does not sap their efforts, but which taints their joy and at times corrodes a part of their courage.

They lacked gratitude to those they despoiled.

Every woman and man, at the outset of their days, stole everything – even the language they speak.

None of the models they imitated was meant for them.

Even the name they bear remains their whole life long a thing they have usurped.

What gives them their being, when they look into themselves deeply, is the shadow of a childhood dependency, which they are so reluctant to accept that they deny even the vestiges of it. This theft within them is already a sin. A sequence of fraud and remorse ensues. Those whose hands are covered in blood manufacture there and then the clear conscience that is really grime added by the passing of time. They deny having been mere nothings. In no instance are they prepared to admit it. Against the armies of memories too painful, they raise fortresses and walls of hollow language.

Cicero, Seneca, great statesmen and Stoic ascetics, millionaire princes, were the masters of sermonising. Meeting a sermoniser in one's life immediately fills one's soul with shame.

The opposite of Cicero was Caelius.[xliii]

So it is, sadly, that those whose hands are the cleanest are more anxious, being at the same time more innocent. Since lucidity does not tear out its own eyes, those with their eyes widest open have more tears.

Chapter XLV

Giordano Bruno

The Earth ceased to be the cosmological fulcrum of the universe. In an instant, human history was no longer at the centre of time. The most intense moment of the Baroque Age is the sacrifice of Bruno in the flames at Rome on the Campo de' Fiori, beneath the gaze of Schoppius on 17 February 1600, the learned man's body having itself become a flame.

Become a flower in the flames leaping towards the sun.

The heavens no longer revolved about the Earth.

A cultivated, scholarly man died for this new dance in the immense darkness of the void of space.

*

Alexandre Koyré wrote marvellously that over the course of the seventeenth century, the veil of Saint Veronica became torn forever.

Mademoiselle tore it still further to pieces by inventing, in the Luxembourg Palace, the portrait; Saint-Évremond, by inventing the short treatise; Pascal, the fragment; La Rochefoucauld, the dark maxim; and Madame La Fayette, the French novella.

*

On Monday 25 July 1661, the *procureur du roi* and the *lieutenant civil* betook themselves to Port-Royal de Paris at half past six in the morning. They left their carriage and walked round the building to make certain there was no hidden door to the sanctuary they were about to cordon off. They returned to the main gate, knocked gently and, without warning, grabbed the extern nun on duty. Gripping her by the arm and dragging her along, they made her take them to all those with quarters overlooking the courtyard. They began by entering the home of Madame de Sablé, who was still in bed. They woke her. And moved on to Monsieur de Sévigné and then to Mesdemoiselles d'Atri and Gadeau. As they couldn't get into the dwelling of Madame de Guéméné, who was away and had locked up her apartments, they put up a ladder and climbed its rungs to look over the garden wall. They came back down and ordered that Madame de Sablé's two doors be walled up, one looking out onto the courtyard and the other directly into the monastery.

On 18 August 1661 the doors to Madame de Sablé's apartment were walled up.

*

What is Jansenism? The incredible invention of a 'society of solitaries'.

Six leagues from Paris, women lived as a group in an abbey. One by one, men sporadically left the city to live with them, revolving around their retreat, their silence, their solitude, like satellites circling this strange female sun. In no way, however, did they mean to enter the group or swear allegiance to it. They had no desire to be monks. They preferred to stay on the boundary between worlds, and favoured the periphery of the building, lurking around the granges, far from the madding crowd, resolutely fleeing the pack of wolves on the one hand, yet on the other not dubbing themselves hermits or anchorites, but *solitaires*. In addressing each other, they made concessions to ritual but remained secular, using the title Monsieur. Antoine Le Maistre took advantage of the situation to learn Hebrew: he was the first solitary. Then came Monsieur de Séricourt and Monsieur de Bascle.

*

On 18 October 1684, the Edict of Nantes is revoked.

On 28 January 1710, Port-Royal des Champs is razed to the ground.

The dispersal of the *solitaries* was decreed.

How can you disperse solitude?

Chapter XLVI

Madeleine de Sablé

The Marquise de Sablé's worldview is one of extraordinary, anxious sadness.

She had a phobic hatred of death.

Fear of the final expulsion of breath and, most importantly, the contagion of the air that followed, was the greatest of her terrors.

She detested nature, rusticity, fields, Port-Royal des Champs, ponds, flowers, fruit trees: what she called 'the foul country air'.

Her greatest dread was of losing her sense of smell.

She would burn juniper wood whenever a death was announced. She passed the letters she received over the flames to disinfect them. She avoided anyone with a cold and went to her room whenever she heard sneezing at her door. She said the nose was the body's most powerful sense organ. She was passionate about the attractions of soups and the delights of jams. She had recipes for all the delicacies. Despite a *sablé* today being, thanks to her, the name of a sweet biscuit, melancholia followed her everywhere, notwithstanding all the flaky pastry she filled with egg yolks and caster sugar. She could not bear the use of the second person singular in books of poetry. The sight of dirty ornamental pools offended her. Her name for all the sounds made by the mouth, and for all the faces one sometimes pulls – jowls puckered and hollowed around the teeth – when one eats, chews and swallows, was 'mortalities'. She launched Jansenism. She launched La Rochefoucauld. She launched Pascal. In 1665, at the height of the persecution of Port-Royal, when La Rochefoucauld published – revised by him and approved by her – the fragments of caustic sentences that he had elaborated with Jacques Esprit's collusion, she distributed copies and brought her influence to bear on the host of women who had loved the duke, with the exception of Madame de Longueville, whom he had wounded too deeply after giving her a child, and of Madame de Lafayette, who was not yet definitively enamoured of him, even though he was beginning to frequent her circle. Lastly, Madame de Sablé wrote a review of La Rochefoucauld in the first, and at that point only, literary periodical of the day, which had begun to appear that year. The *Journal des Savants* published the article by Madeleine de Souvré de Sablé on the kinds of maxims invented by

François de La Rochefoucauld on 9 March 1665.

*

In 1673, when Jacques Esprit's immense, interminable book was at last ready to go to press, Madame de Sablé was keen to publish, at the same time and in direct competition to it, her own collection of maxims. The approval, licensing, registration and printing took four years. In 1678, the printers' presses at last produced the two works. But by the time the books appeared, their authors were dead. There was no one to speak up for them. Their publication scarcely made a ripple on what had become the indifferent surface of time.

Chapter XLVII

A Carrot Soup

'It is never right to scorn death.'

*

To Madame de Sablé: 'Here are all the maxims I have; but since one does not do anything for nothing, I ask of you a carrot soup.'

*

'Neither the sun nor death can be looked upon with a steady eye.'

La Rochefoucauld, like Freud, says yes to the end that holds sway over our days; says yes to everything; says yes to the baseness of the world. A strange rock located deep in his name[xliv] de-petrifies the petrifying Medusa. La Roche Foucauld means the rock or stone that sits atop the site. Paul Hazard writes of his work:

it is 'the most difficult of the seventeenth century'. Stendhal meditated on it. Taken up again by Nietzsche, it feeds into the thinking of Bergson and Heidegger. A labyrinth leading to a darkness that leads to the abyss. His whole life long, Jacques Lacan repeated everywhere that strange maxim of La Rochefoucauld's, which he imputed to the intrusion of language into human life: 'There are people who would never have been in love if they had never heard speak of it.'

*

La Rochefoucauld writes to Madame de Sablé: 'To Madame de Sablé. Friday evening. Here are all the maxims I have, which you do not. But, since one does not do anything for nothing, I ask of you a mutton stew and a beef stew like the ones we had when Commander de Souvré dined at your table, with *sauce verte*, and another dish, either a capon with prunes or some other you consider worthy. If I could hope for two plates of those preserves that I hardly deserved to eat in times gone by, I would be indebted to you my entire life.'

*

La Rochefoucauld drank his soup, devoured his blackberry and plum preserves, tore down the dead language, exploded the well-balanced, gilded, silvered, bronzed, finely wrought, incense-laden cant of the Counter-Reformation, and dismantled the heavy, ornate phraseology of the previous century's humanism. He turned a sumptuous, oratorical language into a fiery, calcinated one. He transformed balanced, sinuous, augmentative, cyclical forms into sharp, dazzling fragments.

Those fragments, verging upon incredulous silence, are extraordinarily dense aporias.

They are not so much poems as mental propulsions smashing into the reader.

The antlers that stags leave behind after their duels amid the ruddy bracken in the mists of November.

A chrysalis, in Greek, means a golden tunic.

*

It is like a revelling in the worst. A joy in saying yes in spite of everything. This 'yes', simple as it is, translates into a dessication of style. Thinking and ruination were mingled. Civil war and internal conflict were juxtaposed but, all of a sudden, melted into one another in this dense, slender volume of 410 fragments, a tiny 71-page book. These snippets of language are like the slingshot-stones that children pack into their belts before climbing the trees and using them to stun birds. It is the finest book in our language. Almost as profound as the work by Étienne de la Boétie – brilliant, but still so oratorical, Latin, and formally ornate – which likewise calls for the eradication of all monarchy and speaks in praise of tyrannicides.

*

The last maxim in La Rochefoucauld's book begins as follows: 'After speaking of the falsity of so many apparent virtues, it is reasonable to say something about the falsity of scorning death. I mean that contempt for death which pagans boast of deriving from their own strength. I doubt that anyone of good sense has ever believed in it.'

*

La Rochefoucauld: 'Everything is insipid when one has felt love.'

*

There is an I-shall-never-forget-that in love, which is

perhaps something like the true date residing in the depths of the soul. Something like the givenness of the given. There is an extraordinary discharge of electricity in one's feeling that opens one up to the world, opening up the body to the other, binding one to the world, going back to the dazzling instant of birth and, further back still, to the instant uniting bodies in the origin.

*

A strange 'echolocation' of the spoken language in souls.

Voices of those who once were, open up for themselves a passage in the souls of those who outlive them.

Madame de Sévigné wrote wonderfully of La Rochefoucauld: 'His speech felt its way in the air. As he spoke, he was still striving for expression. He tried out words, sought out tones too. He thinks in stops and starts; his sentences touched the air and groped for its substance; palpated the words, the enunciations, the suffixes and prefixes, and endeavoured to recognise their true senses. He was the old, refined, disfigured, gouty samurai, almost reckless in his daring, reaching for a word.'

Chapter XLVIII

La Galigaï

The impressive final scene in which the Marquise d'Ancre *removes her blindfold, then does so again* dates to Saturday 8 July 1617.

La Galigaï wants to see.

This is Dido on the tower at Carthage as Aeneas's ship fades away over the sea.

'Remember me'.[xlv]

She lights the pyre.

La Galigaï was the byname of Leonora Dori, who had become the Marchioness of Ancre by marrying Concino Concini, who himself subsequently became a Marshal of France.

She is led down to the banks of the Seine and taken to her death. She is pushed onto the steps to the pyre. The square on the river is crammed with onlookers. She is blindfolded. Prodded in the back and forced to mount the steps. She climbs to the *eschaffaut* that has been built on the Place de Grève, but once standing on it, she removes her blindfold.

She looks out on the Seine, filled with the boats and gondolas that have gathered. Suddenly she turns around. She looks at the crowd screaming and shouting on the river banks. She was blindfolded again. She protests, saying she is 'desirous of staring both her murderer and death in the face'. The blindfold is put on but she removes it again, using her tied hands. Things speed up at that point. She dies, run through by a sword below her breast before being stripped naked and thrown into the flames.

Chapter XLIX

Spinoza

When we stop loving, when we give up drinking, when we break off the stupefying addiction to a drug, when we wean ourselves off tobacco and off dispersing its perfumed, coloured, unpredictable, delicious smoke into the air, then, beyond the sporadic bouts of agony, beyond the panic states triggered by absence or frustration, we experience some strange, curious moments of *withdrawal euphoria*, moments accompanied by an impression of mental clarity. We suddenly find ourselves so lucid that the human reality around us, and even the noise of animals and vegetation that arises and presses upon us before break of dawn, seem like chimaeras, hydras, gryphons or sphinxes. All of a sudden, even natural things (the form of plants, the grand piano in the living room, finger joints, shiny fingernails, the damp globes of the eyes watching us, the delicate pale cartilage of the auricles listening to us) seem outsized or menacing. Civilised objects (coaches, presidential limousines, wheelbarrows, electric bicycles, sedan chairs, horses, bomber aircraft, curtains and the curtain-loops that hold in the folds of the curtains beside the windowsills – places that cats make their own, the iron canons and their stone cannonballs, swords, their hilts and hilt-guards, their pommels and scabbards, bazookas and the surveillance drones observing the anti-epidemic masks as they move around deserted avenues, the great clocks and their arrow-headed hands rotating up on the clocktowers) seem like total fakery, almost like monsters in the visible world.

Seeing turns to an unexpected state of alarm.

That said, it is not clear why the truth would be a source of euphoria. By what token should it be convincing or benign? In what way should the norm tend, in and of itself, to be profoundly abnormal? Similarly, it is unclear why the real should be understandable. Why should nature be calculable? Why should time be foreseeable? And destiny interpretable? Science gives the false impression of having organised the real at source, so as to be able to claim to explain it. But geometry did not invent the Earth. Mathematics is no cause of the strange circle that the orbits of the stars describe in the sky, nor of vegetal growth, nor of the inverse symmetry of reflections, nor of the division of living cells, nor of the inexplicably sexual multiplication of the beings that populate nature. Psychiatry did not engender the madness that it compartmentalises so insanely, so cruelly itself, and which it tames so little while claiming to master it. The effect of getting closer to truth – of *getting warmer* – is the tearing-up of a distance, *a tearing*, which reaches nothing, and will certainly never reach back to the genesis of its desire. The source of its desire is its birth; then the source of its birth is its conception; then its desire shifts to the embrace of which it is the fruit, yet which it will never see. And, even as it forms, the loop so formed instantly passes out of the range of sight.

It is not, then, lucidity that can be said to be euphoric. The joy of demystification derives more probably from the sadistic, predatory, avid, insatiable, lethal curiosity that precedes it. There is absolutely no exultation specific to seeing clearly or darkly or unfogged or without tears or seeing true. The pleasure of piercing the veil goes back to the voyeurism specific to animal sight: to the desire to have one's eyes converge on the impossible scene at its source, on the ultimate scene at its end. The inexpressible joy of seeing the prey falling to its death to feed one's hunger.

*

I love this sense of a blindfold being untied, of a scarf being removed, of freedom and light.

*

Though excommunicated, rejected by his family, banished from his community in a sinister ceremony with candles extinguished, cornets sounded, disownment, disinheritance and escheat declared, and his writings banned – he did not embrace Christianity. He did not join the philosophers.

Spinoza: 'Non sum philosophus.'

Benedictus Spinoza said he preferred fights between spiders to the disputes of the theologians of Rome; to the hair-splitting of the rabbis of the remarkably touching, ancient and small synagogue on the Island of Djerba (amid the troupes of pink flamingos and the whiteness of the sea salt); to the metaphysical dialogues of Athens; to the celestial ladders of Byzantium's Platonists perilously erected beneath the cosmic vault.

A *textum* stowed away in the cupboard *sine nomine*.

A 'text' one cannot publish without dying there and then, a text to be hidden away, one that *bides its time*.

Spinoza corresponded with Saint-Évremond, resident then in the parish of St. James in London and a friend of Hobbes and Jean de la Fontaine. In 1673 Spinoza replied to the Elector Palatine that he 'had never thought of becoming a professor of philosophy.'[xlvi] He denied having written books, but not having contemplated doing so.[xlvii] From his family and the house in which he was born, he had retained only a 'very fine bed with case curtains attached, convenient for reading.' He polished enormous magnifying lenses to have a closer view of the world. They called him *infelix litterator* while he himself remained silent. He was also called *irreligiosus auctor*, and that expression is a wonderful challenge for the mind even if no one on Earth can entirely achieve the aim, so much do hopes, memories of sensory joys, dreams and prayers spontaneously fire the circuits of the brain when night falls and the body descends into sleep. He himself said it, repeated it, proved it: *anima est fascinata* (the psyche is blinded by the hallucinatory dream in which it has its origin). It is difficult to break free of the enigma of one's earliest days. We dreamt even before we emerged into the day and discovered its light. It is perhaps impossible to extricate one's style from the incomprehensible hummings of one's infancy. There is no point hoping to unravel our preferences from the addiction of our first mouthfuls. It takes extraordinary effort to retrace, one by one, the slow stages of domestication; to disentangle oneself from the powerful impressions of custom in order, if not to free oneself from them, then at least to have such fetters *somewhat* removed, to see them almost *dissolved.* How are we to divest ourselves of the hulls, scales, pelts and contours of judgements, of the skins, fangs and talons of the words of our forefathers' language? Who can wholly escape the abyss of a body that has sheltered you, the Egypt of a world that has enslaved you? Freedom would be to dodge the abyss. But who can free himself from death? Who is free? It is possible only to free oneself *a little.*

*

It is the arm of the boy of Ingolstadt bursting through the layer of earth where his mother buried him and thrusting again toward the sky.[xlviii]

*

Rawness bespeaks more than nudity. The naked wildens itself, as though there were a *rawness* behind nudity. Behind sense there is something sensory. There is an intense pleasure in the spectacle of wildness that further heightens it. Look at the cat and the mouse. Look at the cat and the bird. There is an *askesis* in bringing the argument down as far as the feet. And right to the ends of dirty claws and almost to hoof level. There is even an *ekstasis* in disabling the symbolic dimension, which is distinct from the desire for truth that is of the order of the imaginary.

Truth has to do only with the true and the false.

Rawness poses questions of genealogy and phylogenesis – that is to say, Genesis – which is always the primal curiosity, which is the primal scene of truth.

The British use the expression 'sleeping in the raw' for sleeping without nightclothes.

So I am suddenly back with the Apostle Paul, the apostate, the deserter, with his two hands still feeling their way as he gradually recovers his sight in the basket as it is let down from along the city walls of Damascus. The man is *de-scaled.* The mysterious 'scales' have fallen from his eyes. The remains of fish scales in our bodies are our twenty finger- and toenails at the end of our third digital bones or phalanges. Then he says: All things are naked in God's sight.[xlix] *Omnia nuda.* Everything is naked. All things are naked.

Chapter L

Plutarch

Plutarch at Rome argued that the goddess Aletheia was not just 'shrouded' in light: she *was* a chaos of light. Writing of the brilliance that characterises the manifestation of truth – in the palace of the emperor who has provided him with lodgings in the reconstructed city, where he produces in Greek the profoundest pages of late Roman antiquity – he tells that, because she appears through that blaze of light, her face is blurred by it. The blaze of light does not prevent her from being recognised; simply, her features cannot be made out. This is not because the goddess is veiled: she is naked, but the desire for her nudity fascinates us and disrupts the lineaments of her body. It is our gaze that has been disturbed, dazzled by the radiance of the star, irradiated by the concupiscence inflaming it, stupefied by the difference it senses. Its desire has grown so obsessive that the whole body is now erect. It is the whole body dreaming on its feet.

Only the dead (those who have no desire) see what is unveiled, the naked truth, and that takes us to the Underworld. The maw that opens. To Chaos, the first god in chronological order, and to nothing. Darkness. Diaphanous, shadowless perception, free from voracity and shorn of curiosity, is unknown to humans, to animals, to birds, to the wild animals that persist in ancestors, ghosts, demons and gods. They are all too hungry not to glimpse something of the silhouette they hope to see in the light they bring, a light relayed by their own gaze. Truth projects no trace of itself into the world of the living (where all is contoured surfaces, sensation, image, desire), nor into the heads of humans (subject to the sexual alterity by which their conception is governed; to the abaliety of their origin; to what succeeds in hiding from them the death toward which they are heading; to the dreams at night when behind the closed shells or scales of their eyelids they so marvellously see what drives their hunger and their thirst; to the dissent of words learnt from the phantoms of the dead that linger unsteadily in the depths of their souls).

*

The vicinity of the origin is a dark region. It is too

dense for the mind. The mind cannot conceive it. It melts.

*

Being born, living, reproducing and dying constitute a 'fortune' – a mix of good and bad fortune – beyond our control and as strange to bear over its full duration as it is disconcerting to live each of its instants. I have seen people I loved dying from the idea of dying. Wrecking, devastating their lives from the idea of dying. We can, of course, decide our life's end point, provided we get out ahead of it. We can steal a march on the line to be crossed to take us back to formlessness, but cannot remedy its strangeness by planning to catch it unawares. The evil in our societies is less remarkable than life on Earth. Even death is less strange. Nature is the wonder of this world. And the nudity of desiring bodies alerts, surprises, depraves and delights even more than do life, rivers, shorelines, birdsong, mountains, clouds and snow. Women and men are astounded to be women and men pursuing, the whole world over, a frenzy, a sweetness, a longing, an endless, tirelessly polarised rivalry with each other, aided by reproduction and by death – and yet against death, for their conflict, in the flow of their pleasures, renews the society they create – expanding it in the most poignant, most individual face-to-face to be had in the experience of our time. Jacques Esprit wrote:

> Poets never tire of exaggerating the audacity of the first men who took it upon themselves to cross the seas and who, contenting themselves with putting a few fragile planks between themselves and death, found paths and tracks through the fathomless deep. For my part, I find those who first formed the intention of living in society much more audacious; and I am certain that he who has never felt extreme astonishment at that undertaking has never considered it, or knows nothing of the nature of men, who, far from having the requisite qualities for uniting, have all those needed to persecute each other, tear each other limb from limb, destroy each other. If someone finds it difficult to believe it generally true that the nature of man is proud, fierce and inhumane, he has only to cast his eyes over every part of the world; he will see that the rich and the powerful everywhere oppress the poor and the unprotected; he will see that men boast everywhere of the advantages their male sex gives them over the female. All the world's polities are based on violence, the submission to a father figure, slavery and the fine phrases of those

who dominate others. Murderers and criminals are broken on the wheel, yet they are to be seen daily butchering innocents on the public highway, often to meet no need, but merely to satisfy their cruel inclinations. As Montaigne puts it, nature has, I fear, attached to man some instinct for inhumanity.

*

'No thought, no philosophy is necessary in itself', wrote Henri Bergson at the end of the introduction to *La Pensée et le Mouvant*.[1] Then he added this sublime sentence: 'No one is ever required to write a book.' There is a suffocating – natal – ecstasy at the play of chance that is the first impression life offers upon the alarming exit from every mother's vulva. Constantly, on the borders of horror as while we are being born, thought and language fail us before the indescribable real – a real so raw, uncivilised and radiant in the violent ambit of the star that seethes and illuminates. The frames that regiments it and the fortuitous linguistic code that puts in order those frames fissure at times; the apparent order and its placid, extremely differentiated hierarchies allow Night through the breach: Nyx the daughter of the formless infinite Chaos, from whom even the senses flee. Thought then becomes catastrophic. Or eschatological. Or rather, it is a rhetoric that breaks down the current discourse, that interrupts its ceremonial parades and its empty appointments, that stops its endless rounds, that becomes the destroyer of hypnotising faith. It sweeps away the hopeful expectation that will not let go of the ancestral, immemorial reverie which dreaming, in birds and mammals, has mysteriously nourished.

Truth is not primal like that Night. It is a disabusing; it is a depravation; it is a despair. It de-falsifies. It is simply the joy of at last feeling what feels. A joy of disillusionment. That disenchantment, *désideration*, is an ecstasy. The truth is always a demystification presupposing the mystification at its foundation, which it gradually lays bare. It is a joy in denuding. Every society survives through self-mystification about its functioning, so as to ensure its durability and in the hope of concealing its markedly sexual nature (its division at the very heart of joy) and self-destructibility (the war which both grounds that society and claims, in unspeakable fashion, to defend it; which struggles importunately to distract it from the end of the world it has set in motion). What would the truth be that were not first deceptive so that we could be disabused of it? Each new truth can only emerge from a truth-rejection greater than the truth that it is un-deceiving, un-deluding, un-dazzling and un-fascinating, that it is wresting from imaginary fantasy. This truth necessarily sidesteps the whole presupposed by the piece of otherness it is bent on stripping bare. The genus Homo invented incredible forms of suffering for the human bodies that made up the different species, then the different groups, then the different states, to protect itself from the knowledge of death. Behind what the Neanderthal or Sapiens called the real, there stands 'the untamed', which was lost in spoken languages or repressed by forming hordes fleeing from lands, islands, mainlands or even flying into space. Hence, the real is more unpredictable than living creatures themselves. We have no more precise image of the origin than a relic radiation emitted three hundred and eighty thousand years after the strange flash of the first implosion. The unforgettable is bigger than the truth, and the originary vaster than the unforgettable.

There are no notes in the original work.
The following are the translator's notes.

[i] *Noche Oscura*, a poem of 1578 or 1579, from which the phrase 'Noche oscura del alma' – the dark night of the soul – derives. The treatise *Ascent of Mount Carmel* is, in part, a commentary on the poem.

[ii] Until January 1993, French parents were allowed to give their children 'traditional' names only. In practice, this meant names of Christian saints or, less commonly, names from classical antiquity.

[iii] Because Quignard plays extensively on the etymology of the French word *Jadis*, when I first translated this term more than a decade ago, I coined the term 'the Erstwhile' to cover a range of its usages and associations. At its most straightforward, this quasi-neologism designates what Quignard calls 'what is out of memory, that "past before what came to pass", the language-less time prior to biography, the animal time prior to history' (Quignard, *The Sexual Night*. London: Seagull Press, 2014, 18). In that same work, he argues that 'In Old French, *jadis* breaks down into *ja y a dies* – already there was a day', going on to translate this into what he admits is an 'almost incomprehensible' sequence of words: 'Already, in the past, there was there is' (ibid., 158). This etymology arises again in this work at page 186.

[iv] I have followed Pascal Quignard's French translation here: 'Les vieux ont beau vieillir, toutes choses sont neuves'. The King James Bible version of this passage is: 'Old things are passed away; behold, all things are become new' (2 Cor. 5:17).

[v] King Louis IX of France.

[vi] The *male marée* – the bad or evil tide – of 1525 was the first major disaster to strike Le Havre, which had only been founded in 1517. It wreaked considerable havoc, leading to much rebuilding and a re-thinking of the town's sea defences.

[vii] In 1748 Carl Linnaeus developed the idea of a flower clock, *horologium florae*, by which flowers, as they opened or closed, would tell the time of day.

[viii] A reference to the legend of Philomela, Procne, Tereus and the boy Itys in Ovid's *Metamorphoses*.

[ix] I have followed Quignard's French text here. Translations into English are commonly simpler in structure, e.g. Sir Richard Jebb: 'All things the long and countless years first draw from darkness, and then bury from light; and there is nothing which man should not expect' (*The Ajax of Sophocles*. Edited with introduction and notes by Sir Richard Jebb. Cambridge: Cambridge University Press, 1893).

[x] In English in the original.

[xi] *Ethics* V, 27, scholium.

[xii] Ibid., V, 42, scholium.

[xiii] Published in English in 1706 as *Discourses on the Deceitfulness of Human Virtues*.

[xiv] Le sieur de Blancheroche or Blancrocher was the lutenist Charles Fleury (c. 1605–1652). The civil disorder in question was an incident in the Fronde.

[xv] This is the English name for what was known in French as 'la journée du Feu'.

[xvi] La Rochefoucauld's phrase about rivers and the sea occurs in no. 171 of the 1678 edition of his *Maximes* (Paris: Garnier, 1967, 44).

[xvii] The name translates as Hedgehog.

[xviii] From *The Peloponnesian War*, Book 1, Chapter 22.

[xix] Pascal Quignard published *L'être du balbutiement: Essai sur Sacher-Masoch* in 1969.

[xx] A reference to the first supplement to La Rochefoucauld's *Maxims* in the 1665 edition: 'Here then is the picture of self-love whereof the whole of our life is but one long agitation. The sea is its living image; and in the flux and reflux of its continuous waves there is a faithful expression of the stormy succession of its thoughts and of its eternal motion.'

[xxi] Known today as the Küçük Menderes or Little Meander.

[xxii] This is a remark from a letter of 8 October 1936, in response to a lecture delivered by Binswanger in Vienna in honour of Freud's 80th birthday.

[xxiii] Baisao (1675–1763), a monk of the Obakus school of Zen Buddhism, was famous for selling tea in Kyoto.

[xxiv] The book was translated into English as *Essays in Idleness*.

[xxv] At Villeneuve-lès-Avignon.

[xxvi] In addition to 'mort' meaning dead in French, the Breton word 'mor' means sea.

[xxvii] These words, in English in the original, are the title of a book by Darby English, published by MIT Press in 2007.

[xxviii] Johann Jakob Froberger (1616–1667). The piece in question, also known as the 'Memento Mori Froberger', was not published in his lifetime.

[xxix] 'Qui est aussi mal-heureux qu'il croit ? Qui est aussi heureux qu'il l'avait espéré ?' This echoes La Rochefoucauld's

'On n'est jamais si malheureux qu'on croit, ni si heureux qu'on avait espéré', one of the items deleted from the second edition of his major work. (See 'Maximes supprimées : 1. Maximes retranchées après la première édition', La Rochefoucauld, *Maximes*, Paris: Garnier Frères, 1967, 137).

[xxx] It was in 1936 that the Danish seismologist Inge Lehmann discovered the Earth's solid inner core, sometimes referred to by French geophysicists as *la graine*, which, in everyday parlance, means seed.

[xxxi] The architect Ange-Jacques Gabriel designed the Royal Opera House at Versailles, which was opened on 16 May 1770.

[xxxii] Published by Patrice Trigano in 1994.

[xxxiii] The French edition was published by Chandaigne in 1992.

[xxxiv] Published by Gallimard, 2022.

[xxxv] See above, note xv.

[xxxvi] In some European folklore, swallows are said to use celandine to restore sight to their chicks.

[xxxvii] In Latin: *Via recta*.

[xxxviii] Acts 9: 18.

[xxxix] The practice of dressing toddlers of both sexes in skirts persisted in France into the 1950s. The reference to silks perhaps suggests ceremonial occasions.

[xl] Now called the Jardin du Palais-Royal.

[xli] Charles Perrault publishes the most famous version of 'Bluebeard' in his *Histoires ou contes du temps passé* of 1697.

[xlii] The phrase 'Surdum est' was used by Thomas Hobbes in his *De Corpore* (1655) to critique the theological maxim 'Credo quia absurdum' (I believe because it is absurd). Hobbes dismisses the theological maxim as being deaf to reason and logic.

[xliii] Marcus Caelius Rufus (c. 88–48 BC) was a disciple of Cicero in Rome, but a rather more scandalous public figure.

[xliv] *La roche* in French means the rock.

[xlv] The words 'Remember me', referring to the haunting line from 'Dido's Lament' in Purcell's *Dido and Aeneas*, are cited in English in the original.

[xlvi] This seems to be a reference to Spinoza's letter of 30 March 1673 to the Elector Palatine's secretary Fabritius.

[xlvii] Spinoza had published in 1670 his controversial *Tractatus theologico-politicus* under an assumed name.

[xlviii] The story of the dead boy of Ingolstadt, referenced in Quignard's *L'enfant d'Ingolstadt* (Paris: Grasset, 2018), especially pages 194–199, goes back to a Hans Sachs ballad of 1522.

[xlix] 'Omnia nuda et aperta sunt oculis Eius ad quem sermo' (Hebrews 4:13). 'Neither is there any creature that is not manifest in his sight: but all things are naked and opened unto the eyes of him with whom we have to do.' (King James Bible)

[l] In English: *The Creative Mind: An Introduction to Metaphysics*. Translated by Mabelle L. Andison (New York: Philosophical Library Inc., 1946).